CRIME BITERS!

BITERS!

FANGS FOR EVERYTHING

CRIME BITERS!

FANGS FOR EVERYTHING

TOMMY GREENWALD
WITH ILLUSTRATIONS BY ADAM STOWER

| SCHOLASTIC PRESS | NEW YORK

Library of Congress Cataloging-in-Publication Data available

ISBN 978-1-338-19328-2

10 9 8 7 6 5 4 3 2 1   19 20 21 22 23

Printed in the U.S.A.   23
First edition, February 2019

Book design by Yaffa Jaskoll

TO THE REAL-LIFE SUPERHEROES
WHO DEFEND OUR COUNTRY

AN EXTREMELY BRIEF HISTORY OF THE CRIMEBITERS

Case File #1: The Bad Babysitter

Jimmy Bishop adopts a dog, Abby. He soon realizes that she's a crime-fighting superhero vampire dog. Jimmy forms the CrimeBiters with his best friend, Irwin Wonk; his new ~~crush~~, I mean, friend, Daisy Flowers; and of course Abby. Together, they solve the Case of the Bad Babysitter and help catch the perpetrators, Barnaby Bratford and his sister, the evil Mrs. Cragg. Then they make friends with Barnaby's son, the former bully Baxter Bratford, and he becomes the fifth CrimeBiter.

Case File #2: The Rotten Rival

Jimmy's parents make Abby go to obedience school, where she becomes much better behaved but also more like other dogs. Jimmy doesn't like that very much. Jimmy joins the lacrosse team. Irwin doesn't like that very much. Daisy makes a new friend named Mara. Jimmy and Irwin don't like that very much. Baxter is on the lacrosse team too, but Jimmy quickly becomes better than him. Baxter doesn't like that very much. Then a bunch of kids on the team start getting hurt, and no one likes that very much. Luckily, the CrimeBiters discover someone is trying to hurt the kids on purpose, solve the Case of the Rotten Rival, and save the day—and everyone likes that very, very much.

Oh, and Mrs. Cragg turns out to be nice.

Go figure!

Case File #3: The Krazy Kitty

Daisy adopts a cat named Purrkins. Have you ever heard that expression "fighting like cats and dogs"? It was probably invented by people watching Abby and Purrkins, because they did not get along well at *all*. Meanwhile, Baxter is in danger of failing math, and someone tries to shut down Shep's shelter, where Jimmy adopted Abby, by causing a terrible flood. This calls for the CrimeBiters! Eventually, Baxter passes the big test, the gang saves the shelter, and most shockingly of all, Abby and Purrkins become best buddies!

INTRODUCTION

THE BAD GUYS were getting away.

"Faster, Abby!" I yelled. "You have to go faster!"

Abby, my superhero crime-fighting vampire dog, was running like a gazelle on springs. But the bad guys were on a giant motorized skateboard, and it flew through the air at record speed. They looked back at us and cackled sarcastically through their giant orange beards. "You'll never catch us now, losers!"

Daisy Flowers, who was my neighbor, good friend, fellow CrimeBiter, and the most perfect human being on earth, grabbed my hand tightly. "Jimmy, we need you to save the day! You can do it!" Irwin Wonk and Baxter Bratford, the other two members of our gang, nodded desperately.

"Come on, Jimmy, you have to do something!" pleaded Irwin.

"We're all counting on you!" added Baxter.

I pointed ahead. "It's all up to her now," I said. We gazed far into the distance, where somehow, some way, Abby was gaining on the villains. Then, in a flash, she leaped about twenty feet in the air and landed on the back of their skateboard.

"WHAAAA?" cried the culprits, in shock. They tried to smack Abby with the giant spear they were carrying, but Abby kept dodging them. Then ROAARRR! Out came her giant fangs.

"Are you kidding me?" one of the evildoers yelled. "What is she, some kind of magic freak dog?"

I smiled. Pretty much, I said to myself.

The other meanie, who was driving, decided his only chance was to swerve back and forth, trying to get Abby to go flying off the back of the skateboard. But her powerful claws latched onto the guy's black leather jacket. With her hind legs, she kicked both of the perpetrators in the stomach, then clamped her fangs down on the driver's right arm.

"ARRRGHHHH!" the malfeasant screamed. He took his eyes off the road for just a second, and that was all it took to send them crashing into the thicket of bushes, trees, and dirt.

I felt a jolt in my stomach. "Oh no! Abby might be hurt!"

All four of us CrimeBiters sprinted to where the skateboard had gone off the road. We split up and plowed through the branches and bushes, trying to find them.

"Over here!" called Baxter. "They're over here!"

We rushed to where he stood in a small clearing. Baxter pointed down, and there were the two lawbreakers, *sprawled on the ground, their ill-gotten goodies strewn around them.*

And lying right on top of them? None other than my very own Abby, her white fangs gleaming in the sun and her cape-like streak of black fur shining like a suit of armor.

"We give up," said one of the malefactors. "She's too much for us."

Abby had saved the day! She'd done it again!

I ran up and gave her a giant hug. "You're the greatest crime-fighting superhero vampire dog in the whole world!"

We all started cheering, "Abby! Abby! Abby! Abby!"

Then, amazingly enough, the others changed the chant to "Jimmy! Jimmy! Jimmy!" I couldn't believe it! They were cheering for me!

"Jimmy! Jimmy! Jimmy . . . Jimmy . . . Jimmy . . ."

"Jimmy? Jimmy? Hey, Jimmy, wake up!"

Huh? Where am I?

Oohhhhhhh . . .

I rubbed my eyes. Irwin and Daisy were staring down at me.

"Oh, hey, you guys," I said. "I'm not sure what happened."

Irwin clucked his tongue disapprovingly. "I know what happened. You were supposed to meet us to do

homework an hour ago, but you fell asleep in your front yard."

I looked around and saw Abby snoozing under a big tree. She looked about as far from catching bad guys as you can get. "Uh, yeah, I guess I dozed off. Sorry about that."

"Were you dreaming about Abby?" Irwin said, with an accusing tone to his voice. "You were mumbling in your sleep, saying something like, *'You're the greatest crime-fighting superhero vampire dog in the whole world!'*"

"Really?" I said, feeling a tingle of embarrassment start to crawl up my skin. "That seems hard to believe."

"No, that's exactly what you said," Irwin confirmed.

Daisy smiled sweetly. "I think it's adorable that you still think your dog has crime-fighting vampire superpowers, Jimmy," she said. "Usually people grow out of that kind of stuff, but you're, like, a true believer, which is awesome."

I know she was trying to make me feel better, but it kind of had the opposite effect.

Because I knew what she really thought was that I was behaving like an immature little kid. And I was starting to think she was right.

PART ONE

ALL BARK, NO BITE

CHAPTER 1

PROFILE

Name: Jimmy Bishop

Age: The same age I was in the first book, except maybe a little older

Occupation: President of the CrimeBiters

Interests: See above

PROFILE

Name: Irwin Wonk

Age: Two months older than me, which he loves to mention whenever possible

Occupation: Vice-president of the CrimeBiters

Interests: Wishing he were president of the CrimeBiters

IRWIN WONK AND I have been best friends since as long as I can remember. He also happens to have the most awesome trampoline in all of Quietville.

The two things are not related.

I swear.

The day after my little nap break, I was over at Irwin's house after school, bouncing up and down and telling him my innermost thoughts. "Could you believe Daisy yesterday? She was basically talking to me as if I were three years old and believed in fairy tales. Just because I happen to know that Abby has special qualities! I mean, what's with her?"

But Irwin, who didn't like jumping on the trampoline—I know, what a waste, right?—wasn't even listening to me. He was sitting off to the side, staring down at a brochure. "Holy smokes—Amazing Andy has fourteen different species, and he's bringing them all to my house!"

"Huh? Who?"

"Amazing Andy!" Irwin thrust the brochure in my direction. "He's going to be the entertainment at my birthday party next week!"

"Oh," I said, realizing there was no way Irwin was going to pay any attention to me and my problems.

FACT: When someone is planning their own birthday party, they pretty much don't want to talk about anything else.

I hopped off the trampoline. "Can I see that?"

Irwin handed me the brochure. *AMAZING ANDY AND HIS AWESOME ANIMALS* blared a giant headline. *HE'LL TURN YOUR PARTY INTO A REAL ZOO!* Inside, it said that Amazing Andy and his assistant, Reptile Ron, would bring all sorts of exotic animals right into your own home, where you could observe them, pet them, and even hold them.

"Are you sure this is safe?" I asked, pointing at a picture of a kid holding a giant snake.

Irwin snickered. "Of course it's safe! He's, like, the most popular birthday entertainer in the whole state!"

"Well, it sounds pretty cool," I said, feeling a little annoyed that my last birthday party featured a miniature water slide and not much else. I suddenly had a thought that cheered me up. "Hey, can Abby come? She would totally love to see all these awesome animals!"

"Is that a joke?" Irwin snorted. "Absolutely not. That's, like, the worst idea ever."

"It is NOT," I insisted, even though I pretty much knew it was.

Irwin gazed dreamily up to the sky. "Now I just have to decide what kind of cake I want. Originally I was thinking ice cream, but then I remembered Isaac makes a coconut chocolate cream pie that is absolutely to die for."

"To die for? What does that mean?"

Irwin rolled his eyes. "It means delicious. Everyone knows that."

I rolled mine right back. "Well, I definitely think you should go the Isaac route." Isaac was this genius baker who started out at the farmer's market but had recently opened his own small shop in downtown Quietville.

If you've never had one of his chocolate chip cookies, you're missing out on one of the great joys in life.

"I'll think about it," Irwin said, as if he were making a decision that would change the course of human history.

"You do that," I said. Sometimes best friends can be annoying. Especially when they are planning their own birthday parties.

BZZZZ! Irwin's phone buzzed with a text. He looked at it, and his eyes went wide with excitement. "It's Daisy!" I immediately checked my phone to see if she'd texted me too. She hadn't. My annoyance turned into stronger annoyance.

"What does she want?"

Irwin held his phone close to his chest as if it held some sort of top secret message. "She wants to know what we're up to."

I felt a bit of relief in my chest. At least she didn't think I was too immature to hang around with. Phew.

Irwin started typing. "Not much . . . Why . . .?"

He hit SEND, and we both sat there, not saying a word. There was no point trying to pretend to have a conversation when all we wanted to know was what Daisy was going to say next.

BZZZZ!

We stared at Irwin's phone.

WHY DON'T YOU GUYS COME DOWN TO THE BOYS BASKETBALL GAME? I'M HERE!

We both scratched our heads at the same time.

"Why would she want us to go down to the basketball game?" Irwin asked. "And what's she doing there?"

"Beats me." I hopped back up onto the trampoline. If we were going to meet Daisy at the game—and I was pretty sure we were—then I wanted to get a few last jumps in.

FACT: If Daisy Flowers asks you to do something, chances are very, very good that you're going to do it.

Irwin gathered up all his birthday preparation materials. "What color balloons do you think I should have?" he yelled out to me, but I pretended not to hear him.

CHAPTER 2

I'M A GOALIE at lacrosse—and a pretty good one, if I do say so myself—but other than that, sports and I don't get along too well. And basketball? Well, let's just say that the last time I made a basket in gym, the whole school celebrated with a marching band and a ticker tape parade.

I guess what I'm trying to say is, I'm pretty much the last guy you'd expect to show up at a basketball game. To play in, *or* to watch.

And by the way, everything I just said? That goes double for Irwin.

But there we were, walking into the Quietville Recreation Center, which was filled with kids, parents, friends, and relatives, all of whom *loved basketball.*

It felt like entering a foreign country where I didn't speak the language.

The first thing I saw was Chad Knight running down the floor with the ball.

PROFILE

Name: Chad Knight

Age: He looks 12, but he plays sports like he's 28

Occupation: Winning at everything

Interests: Basketball, soccer and, believe it or not, ballroom dancing

Chad, who was the best lacrosse player on our team until he gave it up for ballroom dancing, was a total basketball stud. He looked like a man among boys out there.

"Go to the hoop!" yelled the coach. "You got this!"

Chad whirled, twirled, spun around, and stopped. Then he faked a shot, which made the guy covering him practically jump out of his shoes. Chad watched the defender fly by, then calmly passed to his teammate, John D'Agostino, who made an easy layup.

"That's the way!" the coach exclaimed as everyone in the gym roared. "Great play!"

The cheerleaders went into their post-basket cheer:

"What a shot! What a score! Now all we want is a whole lot more!"

I shook my head. "Is there anything goofier than cheerleading? Standing there, jumping around, yelling 'you're the best' to a bunch of kids you barely know?"

"I don't know," Irwin said. "You seem to like it a lot when they're cheering for you at the lacrosse games."

I didn't respond, which was my way of saying *Good point.*

Irwin squinted, which he did a lot, even though he wore glasses. "Hey, wait a second. *Whoa.*"

"*Whoa* what?"

He pointed across the gym. "*Whoa* that."

I looked. Then I rubbed my eyes. Then I looked again.

No.

It can't be.

There, right in the middle of the cheerleaders I was just making fun of, was none other than Daisy Flowers.

That's right.

Our Daisy Flowers.

"No way," I said.

"Yes way," Irwin answered.

"But she hates cheerleading."

"Guess not."

Without another word, I started making my way over to the other side of the gym. Irwin trailed behind me, asking, "What are you going to do? What are you going to say?" But I didn't answer. There was this weird feeling starting to bubble up inside me, and I had no idea why. All I knew was, it wasn't good.

I waved at a few kids and a few parents I recognized, but I didn't stop to chat. As we got closer, Daisy's friend Mara Lloyd, who was also a cheerleader, spotted us first. She tugged on Daisy's sleeve. "Look! It's Jimmy and Irwin!"

Daisy's face broke out into a big smile. "You guys made it! Yay!"

PROFILE

Name: Daisy Flowers

Age: When you're perfect, does it really matter?

Occupation: Occupying my thoughts way too much of the time

Interests: Cheerleading, apparently

I was too shocked to speak, but Irwin covered for me. "We sure did," he said. "We were wondering why you wanted us to come down to the basketball game, but now we get it."

Daisy grinned again. "Well, yup. Here I am."

I was finally ready to talk. "What's this all about? This is pretty much the last place I expected to find you, and the last thing I expected you to be doing." As I listened to myself, I realized I sounded like a father scolding his child. But I couldn't help it.

"I know, right?" Daisy let out a slightly embarrassed giggle. "I've always thought cheerleading was ridiculous. I mean, why should girls cheer for boys, if boys don't cheer for girls? That's hardly fair."

"So why are you doing it, then?"

Daisy shrugged. "My mom is kind of making me. She said I had to be more physically active. She wanted me to play a sport, but I'm not really a big sports person, so we compromised on this." Daisy grabbed Mara's hand. "Besides, I have some friends on the squad, so it's kind of fun."

"Kind of?" squealed Mara. "It's, like, the most fun ever!"

I rolled my eyes, which Daisy caught. "What?" she said. "What's so bad about it? You love the cheerleaders at your lacrosse games, right?"

"That's what I said!" Irwin chimed in. "And besides, I think it's totally cool that you're doing it."

I shrugged. "Whatever." It didn't make sense that I was mad at Daisy for becoming a cheerleader—I didn't even understand it myself—so I definitely wasn't going to make a thing about it.

Just then, the other team came sprinting down the court, and some kid looked like he was about to make a shot. But out of nowhere, Chad came swooping in and swatted the ball out of the kid's hands. Then he grabbed it and stormed down to the other end, where he made a shot from the foul line.

The cheerleaders went nuts, including Daisy.

"Yay, Chad!!!" she hollered. "That was amazing!"

Then they all went into a cheer:

"Chad Knight, he's our man! If he can't do it, no one can!"

Chad ran back down the court, and he looked right at Daisy. She smiled and gave him a little wave. "Great play!" she chirped.

Irwin and I shot each other a look.

FACT: Irwin didn't like it when Daisy paid attention to me. I didn't like it when Daisy paid attention to Irwin. But NEITHER of us liked it when Daisy paid attention to some other boy.

I suddenly understood my negative feelings a whole lot better. In Daisy's eyes, Chad was the hunky basketball star, and I was the little boy who still believed in vampire dogs.

"Uh, you know what, you guys?" I said. "I just remembered, Irwin and I need to go pick up Baxter and head down to Isaac's bakery, you know, to choose a birthday cake for Irwin's party. So, uh, we have to go."

"We do?" Irwin said.

I gave him a look.

"Oh, right," he added. "We absolutely do."

Daisy moaned. "Darn, really? That stinks. We have some pretty cool cheers coming up at halftime that I wanted you guys to see."

"Daisy can do a backflip!" Mara added. "She's really athletic!"

I tried to look disappointed. "Hate to miss it. See you guys later."

"Great job cheering," Irwin said. "Keep up the good work."

"Oh yeah, right," I added quickly. "Really good job."

Daisy looked skeptical. "Thanks," she said. "I think."

As we headed out, I glanced over at Chad, who was drinking water on the sideline. He saw me, waved, and grinned.

I managed to wave back, but I wasn't quite able to pull off the grin.

HALF AN HOUR later, my dad drove Irwin and me over to Baxter's house to pick him up. Abby was hanging out the back window as usual, her bottom lip flapping in the wind. When that happens, I can see her fangs, which are still an awesome sight.

These days though, it was pretty much the only time I got to see them. Unfortunately she hadn't been in a very fang-y mood lately.

But she was still the most awesome dog ever, obviously, and I took her everywhere she was allowed. Since Isaac has a very dog-friendly policy, his bakery had already become one of Abby's favorite places to go.

Baxter came trotting out to the car. "Hey, you guys," he said. He leaned into the back window and scratched Abby's ear. She licked Baxter's hand in appreciation. It was very sweet and adorable, if all you wanted was a dog who licked people's hands. I wanted more than that though. I wanted the dog who made me feel cool, and brave enough to start the CrimeBiters and talk to Daisy in the first place, and not the dog who made me feel silly for thinking she had superpowers.

That's a lot to ask, I know.

Baxter hopped in the backseat. "Hey, Mr. Bishop."

My dad waved into the rearview mirror. "Nice to see you, Baxter." Baxter leaned over the front seat and fist-bumped my dad. The two of them were pretty good buddies, which was pretty impressive when you consider that Baxter's dad once stole my mom's diamond necklace.

"So how was the basketball game?" Baxter asked.

"It was, uh, *interesting*," Irwin said. "Daisy's a cheerleader now."

"Huh," said Baxter, who didn't seem to care all that much. His attitude toward Daisy—meaning he treated her like she was just another person—made absolutely no sense to me.

I nodded. "Yup. She's gone over to the dark side."

Irwin chuckled. "Chad Knight didn't seem to think it was so bad," he said, just because he knew it would irritate me.

"Well, I think it's great," my dad chimed in. "Cheerleading is a time-honored tradition, and a fine one at that."

PROFILE

Name: Baxter Bratford

Age: 13, but don't tell anyone, he gets embarrassed

Occupation: Former bully and the only bald member of the CrimeBiters

Interests: Lacrosse, passing math

"Mom says that cheerleading is ridiculous and sexist and should be banned," I reminded him.

"Banned seems a bit extreme," said my dad, but he didn't argue the basic point.

"I don't get why boys don't cheerlead," Irwin said. "It does seem weird that it's only for girls. I mean, girls and boys play a lot of the same sports, right? So what's the difference?"

"Any boy who joined cheerleading would be laughed out of school, obviously," Baxter said. He seemed a little glum, maybe because Irwin and I hadn't asked him to come to the game. We probably should have, but we were too distracted by Daisy's invitation to remember.

FACT: When you're thinking about the girl you like, sometimes you forget about other things. Like your friends.

"You're probably right about that, Baxter," my dad agreed. "Which is too bad."

"Can we change the subject?" I said. All this cheerleading talk made me think about Chad and Daisy smiling at each other, which was a lot less fun to think about than Isaac's chocolate chip cookies.

"You brought it up," muttered Irwin.

27

"Yeah, well, now I'm bringing it down."

"I know what we can talk about," said my dad, with a little extra pep in his voice. "You guys getting out of the car, because we're here. Pick you up in an hour."

As I opened the car door, my dad grabbed my arm. "You know, Jimmy, just because Daisy cheered for Chad doesn't mean that she actually *likes* him."

I stared at my dad. How the heck did he know exactly what was going on in my head?

"I have no idea what you're talking about," I told him, and I hopped out of the car so fast I could barely hear him giggle and say, "Of course you don't."

CHAPTER 4

FACT: When I grow up, I want to live in a bakery.

BAKE NEWS!—WHICH was the name of Isaac's bakery—had only been open for about two months, but it was already the most popular place in town. The guy was a magician with an oven mitt, and everybody knew it. Plus, like I said, you could bring your dog inside if you wanted to. I don't understand why all stores and restaurants don't have that policy.

FACT: Dogs make people happy. And happy people buy stuff.

"What's up, my good friends?" bellowed Isaac as we walked into his store. Isaac was a pretty enormous guy, so when he bellowed, it was the real deal.

"Cookies all around," I told him, "with a side of milk."

Isaac reached to a tray behind him and plucked out three of the chocolatiest, chippiest cookies I ever saw.

Then he poured three glasses of ice-cold milk. My lips started twitching.

"After we finish our cookies, I'd like to discuss options for my birthday cake," Irwin told him. "It's going to be the most amazing party ever, so I'm going to need some of your finest work."

Isaac winked. "You got it, brother." Then he bent down to say hi to Abby. "Hey there, girl." He gave her some kind of biscuit, which she snapped up. I bet it was delicious.

The four of us went outside and grabbed a table on the sidewalk. Abby nestled underneath my legs, keeping an eye on things in case a stray piece of cookie happened to get loose (like *that* was ever going to happen).

Irwin and I ate about half our cookies in one bite, but Baxter just sat there, staring at his.

"Are you sick?" I asked him. It was the only reasonable explanation.

"Nope," he said.

Irwin and I looked at each other, then back at Baxter. The glum expression still hadn't left his face. Plus, he'd been kind of weird ever since he got in the car—quiet and moody. It occurred to me that something more serious might be upsetting him.

"Is something bothering you?" Irwin asked him.

Baxter nodded. "Thanks for asking, Irwin," he said, which felt like a punch in the gut. I'd thought of it first! Well, I'd thought of it at the same time anyway, and now Irwin got the credit for being the caring one.

QUESTION: Why is it that everything between best friends becomes a competition?

I quickly remembered this was about Baxter. Time to forget about me, for once.

"What is it?" I asked. "This isn't about the basketball game, is it?"

"No, of course not. I don't even like basketball." Baxter let out a heavy sigh. "You guys know I have an older brother named Bennett, right?"

Irwin and I looked at each other again.

"Uh, actually I didn't," I admitted.

"Me neither," Irwin added.

"Oh," Baxter said. He took a tiny nibble out of his cookie. I saw Abby looking up at him as if to say *What is wrong with you? If you don't want it, I'll have it!* I knew exactly how she felt. "Well, that's because he's older than me. A lot older."

"Uh, how old?" Irwin asked, which was the next logical question.

"Twenty-two."

I whistled. Twenty-two was *old*. Like, an actual grown-up. "Jeez. Where does he live?"

"Well, that's the thing," Baxter said. "Bennett hasn't lived at home for a long time. He went to college for a while, and then he dropped out, and then he moved to California for a few years, where I think he lived on a beach or something, and we kind of lost track of him for a while, then a few months ago he told us he joined the army."

"The army?" I said. "Wow. That's amazing."

"So, so cool," Irwin said. "He must be, like, such an awesome guy."

"I guess so. I never got to know him all that well, to be honest. But I miss him a lot." Baxter looked off into space for a second, as if he might find what he wanted to say next somewhere out there. "Anyway, I just found out today that he's going overseas."

"Overseas?" I asked. "What does that mean?"

"It means he's going to fight in a war, dummy," Irwin said.

I immediately felt stupid. "Really?"

"I don't know," Baxter said. "Like, not a war, exactly. But I think maybe to search for bad guys or fight terrorism or something like that."

The three of us sat there silently for a few seconds.

"Your brother sounds like a hero," Irwin finally said, very quietly.

"A total hero," I added, just because.

"Thanks," Baxter said. "I think so too. I just hope he stays safe. My mom's really worried. I guess I am too."

Irwin and I didn't have anything to say to that.

I wasn't sure which way to take the conversation from there, but luckily I didn't have to worry about it for too long, because about five seconds later Baxter pointed and said, "Is that guy actually leaving his car there?"

I looked over and saw a guy parking some kind of fancy sports car in a completely illegal space, blocking a bunch of other cars. It wasn't unusual to see terrible parking jobs in our town, because people were always in such a rush that they didn't care if they were actually following the law or anything, but this was especially ridiculous.

"Holy smokes," Irwin said. "That is so obnoxious."

"Maybe we should say something," I said. It was the kind of thing we would report at our weekly CrimeBiters meetings, but I didn't think any of us had actually ever done anything about it before.

Baxter shook his head. "I don't think so. Let's just eat our cookies and mind our own business this time."

I looked down at Abby, who was snoozing peacefully under the table. I thought about how everyone thought it was silly and immature that I still thought she was a crime-fighting vampire dog. This wasn't exactly the ultimate test, but maybe it would offer some kind of proof to everyone that I was right.

"Hey, Ab, wake up," I whispered to her. She raised her head lazily, wondering what could possibly have been so important that it meant interrupting her nap.

After we all watched the man go into a bank, I said, "When he comes out, I'll just ask why he parked illegally and see what he says."

"Well, hold on a minute. I agree with Baxter," Irwin said. "It's possible the guy doesn't realize what he was doing, and it was just an honest mistake." Irwin was always the last one to confront anyone about anything. Except for me, whom he would confront about everything.

"Whatever, you guys decide," said Baxter, who was clearly still preoccupied by his brother's news.

About five minutes later, the sports car guy came out of the bank. He was wearing a dark suit, a pink tie, and sunglasses that wrapped all the way around his head. He was talking on his phone, loudly. And he obviously thought he was just the most awesome person ever.

I grabbed Abby's leash and got up.

"You're really going to say something?" Irwin asked.

"Yup."

Abby and I walked over as the guy finished his call. "I need you to put the kibosh on that whole deal," he was saying into the phone. "That's all there is to it. Today. No excuses." He hung up and noticed me standing there. "What's up, guy?" Then he noticed Abby. "Make sure that dog doesn't do any funny business on my shoes, capiche?"

I shuffled my feet for a second, then plunged in. "Uh, yeah, hey. I was just wondering if you realized that you were parked illegally. And also, that you were blocking cars from getting out."

The guy glanced around, as if trying to figure out whether this was some sort of joke. "You're kidding, right? I was in there for five minutes."

"Yeah, but still. People do that a lot around here, and it's not considerate to other drivers."

"What are you, like, a junior Boy Scout on patrol?" He took his sunglasses off and cleaned them with his tie, then put them back on. "So did someone try to leave while I was parked there? Is that what you're telling me? If so, where are they? I'll beg their forgiveness."

That was a question I hadn't quite anticipated. "Uh, well, actually no, no one tried to get out or anything. But, uh, if they had wanted to, they couldn't have." I glanced over at Irwin and Baxter, but they were both staring at their milk glasses. Some big help they were.

Sunglasses Guy snickered. "Listen, kid, I don't know who or where your parents are, but if they were here, I'd tell them to make sure their son doesn't turn into one of those annoying types who's always getting in other people's business. Now run along."

I didn't move.

"I said, BEAT IT," the guy hissed, leaning in closer. Then he decided not to wait for me to move, and he brushed past me, lightly knocking into my shoulder. As I fell a few steps backward, I heard Irwin gasp.

I looked down at Abby again, hoping to see some sort of sign that she was going to defend me. A fang, a protective growl, anything! But all she did was look up at me like, *Why are we standing here? I was enjoying my snooze under the table.*

"Please be more careful parking next time!" I yelled, just to get the last word. The guy glanced back, gave me a look of disgust, and jumped in his car. The tires squealed as he drove away.

I walked slowly back to the table, where Irwin and Baxter were staring up at me like they'd seen a ghost.

"Are you okay?" Irwin asked.

"What a total jerk that guy was," Baxter said.

I sat down like everything was hunky-dory. "Oh yeah, totally fine, he barely even touched me." But the truth was, I wasn't totally fine. I was a little shaken up. The guy had actually scared me a little bit. And my dog didn't seem to care at all.

"I need you guys to tell me something," I said. "And please don't laugh."

They both stared at me, waiting.

I took a deep breath. "When I got Abby, I realized pretty soon after that she was different from other dogs."

"Uh, yeah, okay," Irwin said warily.

"And then all this crazy stuff happened, which confirmed it," I went on. "I knew that she was special. That she had unique abilities." I paused. "Like special powers." I paused again. "And one of those powers was that she was a vampire."

I stopped. It sounded so stupid when I said it out loud, even though I believed it with all my heart. Or at least, I *had* believed it with all my heart.

"Right," Irwin said impatiently. "So get to the part where you want us to tell you something."

"Oh yeah." I took another deep breath. "I guess my question is . . . I mean, I know you guys think the Abby thing is crazy and everything, but . . . do you think it makes me seem like, you know, a little kid? Like, really immature and stuff?"

Baxter shrugged. "I hadn't really thought about it," he said. "Not really though."

I could have hugged Baxter right then. But before I could feel all relieved, Irwin chimed in.

"Well, if you want the truth," Irwin said, "it does make you seem kind of, like, you know . . . *younger*, I guess. Especially when compared to . . . oh, I don't know . . .

someone like Chad, who's, like, this big super athlete, running up and down the basketball court."

UGH.

He paused, waiting to see how I'd react. "Does that answer your question?"

"Absolutely," I said, keeping my voice as steady as I could. "Thanks for being honest."

"Sure thing."

I was about to walk into the store and drown my sorrows with more cookies and milk, when I stopped short.

FACT: Just when you think things can't get any more stressful, they always do.

Daisy and her mom were heading straight toward us.

CHAPTER 5

"HEY, LOOK, IT'S Daisy," said Irwin, stating the obvious.

She was still in her cheerleading uniform, of course. The game must have just ended, and here she was, smiling and waving.

"I was wondering if you guys would still be here!" she exclaimed, running up to our table.

"We are," said Baxter, also stating the obvious.

"Cool!" Daisy sat down in the chair I'd been in, while I stood there with Abby, not moving.

Mrs. Flowers smiled. "Hi, Jimmy, it's nice to see you. How are your parents?"

FACT: Other parents always ask about your parents, even though they know the answer is always going to be "They're good, thanks."

"They're good, thanks."

Mrs. Flowers nodded at her daughter. "Shall we go in and get a treat?"

Daisy didn't move. "Do I have to? I'm exhausted from all that jumping and flipping and yelling."

"Ha!" Mrs. Flowers looked at me. "Daisy gave me such a hard time about cheerleading. I told her I was a cheerleader back in my day, and it was really hard and a ton of fun, but she kept insisting it was lame and unathletic and boring. And now look at her—too tired to go inside and get a cookie!"

"Well, I saw her cheer, and she was very good," I said. "You should be very proud."

"Right?" said Mrs. Flowers. "I told her I thought she could be captain of the squad next year if she wanted."

"I bet."

FACT: Kids tend to agree with adults a lot. It's just easier that way.

But Daisy wasn't about to let me off the hook. "Wait a second. Back at the game you said you thought cheerleading was ridiculous. And you said you couldn't believe I would ever be a cheerleader."

"I don't remember saying that," I said dumbly.

"And then you left, like, right away." Daisy narrowed

her eyes. "It's true, I wasn't sure I wanted to be a cheerleader. I thought maybe it was silly. But it turned out to be fun and challenging, and I wanted you guys to come see for yourself." I glanced over at Irwin, who always enjoyed watching me squirm. Daisy went in for the kill. "Do you remember back when you started playing lacrosse, and you got so mad at me when I didn't come to watch you play? How is that any different from this? Are you saying that cheerleading is somehow less worthy than lacrosse? Because that's not fair."

"Very well said," Irwin said.

Daisy grinned. "Thanks."

For some reason, it was the grin that really got to me. Maybe it was because she was acting like everything was just peachy, five seconds after making me feel like a total jerk. Maybe it was because Irwin had just said that Chad was a basketball star and I was a little kid who believed in vampire dogs. Whatever the reason, I suddenly got mad, which can be the only explanation for what I said next.

FACT: Whenever you say something because you're angry, chances are very good you're going to regret it later.

42

"Maybe Chad will come down here too," I said to Daisy. "Then you can cheer really loudly for his amazing ability to eat a cookie."

Daisy's face turned cold. "What is that supposed to mean?"

Irwin must have felt bad, because he tried to bail me out, for once. "Jimmy's just kidding around," he said. "Obviously, you were only cheering for Chad really loudly at the game because he's such a good basketball player." Irwin paused. "I mean, that *was* the only reason, right?"

Daisy stood up so abruptly that her chair fell backward.

"Honey?" said her mom, but Daisy wasn't listening.

"I seriously can't believe how childish you guys are being," Daisy said, through clenched teeth. "When are you going to start treating me like an actual person, instead of some object of fascination?"

Irwin and I looked at each other, then at the ground.

"Do you think it's fun knowing that you both have a crush on me? It's not." Daisy threw up her hands. "It's, like, kind of a pain in the neck, if you want to know the truth. And it's no fun having to worry about whether I'm hurting your feelings all the time, just by living my life, and hanging out with friends, and joining activities. It's like you're two little puppies who just want to be petted all the time or something. So you know what? I really don't care if you watch me cheer or not." She paused for a second, and I thought she was done. But she wasn't.

"You guys need to grow up," she added.

Then she was done.

"What did *I* do?" protested Irwin. "Jimmy was the one who said something, not me!"

What a pal, right?

But Daisy didn't answer him—instead, she just marched into the store. Her mom, who was still standing there, smiled and said, "I'll go talk to her," then hurried in after her daughter.

Baxter took another nibble of his cookie. "Well, I was wondering what could possibly distract me enough that I wouldn't keep worrying about my brother," he said. "Now I know."

CHAPTER 6

I REMEMBER THE first time I read a Jonah Forrester book. I was about eight or nine years old, and my mother had taken me to the library for the thousandth time, hoping I would finally find something I would be interested in. But as usual, my reaction to everything she put in front of me was the same. "No." "Don't think so." "Definitely not." "You're kidding, right?"

Then we turned a corner in the children's section and I saw a big poster that said FANGS FOR COMING TO THE LIBRARY! There was a picture of a man in a dark suit and sunglasses, smiling, with just a hint of a fang sticking out under his top lip.

"Who's that guy?" I asked my mom.

"I don't know, but he's creeping me out," she said.

I kept staring up at him, until a librarian walked over. "That's Jonah Forrester," she said. "He's a vampire, but he uses his powers for the good of mankind. He's the star of a series of wonderful books by the author Elroy Evans. Would you like to see one?"

My mom shook her head. "He's a little young, I'm not sure that's a good—"

"Yes, please," I said.

FACT: Kids are more likely to want to read something if their parents don't want them to read it.

I ended up reading all five Jonah Forrester books in about three months.

Needless to say, Elroy Evans is my favorite author ever. Which is why, when I was lying on my bed later that night trying to get over the embarrassing events at Isaac's bakery, I suddenly had a crazy idea.

I got up, went into the living room, sat down at the computer, and started typing.

Dear Mr. Evans:

I think I am probably your biggest fan. I have read all your books over and over again. I love Jonah Forrester and think he is pretty much the best vampire ever created. I really hope to meet you one day and ask you all about your stories. But in the meantime, I have two very important questions to ask you, since you are an expert: How do you know if someone is a vampire? How can you tell if a vampire might not be a vampire anymore?

Just so you know, this is not about me—I am not a vampire. But I have always thought someone I know is a vampire, and now I'm not sure, so I was just wondering if you could help me solve this mystery. Also, this girl I like thinks believing in vampires is childish, and I would love to prove her wrong.

I hope you write lots more Jonah Forrester books, because my parents always tell me I should be reading new books instead of reading your books over and over again.

Your biggest fan (like I said),
Jimmy Bishop

"What are you doing?"

I whipped around to see my big sister, Misty, standing there. She was wearing a bathrobe and had her hair in curlers.

QUESTION: Do girls know how ridiculous they look when their hair is in curlers?

ANSWER: Yes, but they don't care because it's all worth it in the end.

PROFILE

Name: Misty Bishop

Age: Older than me, which will never not be irritating

Occupation: Student, sister, celebrator of my misfortune

Interests: HER PHONE (all caps intentional)

I quickly tried to X out of the program I was in, but Misty was too quick for me. She slapped my hands away, read my letter, and let out a loud laugh. "Ha! That is adorable!"

FACT: Sometimes adorable doesn't mean "adorable." Sometimes it means, "You've gotta be kidding me."

I closed the computer—a little too late, but I did it anyway. "It's none of your business is what it is."

"Are you actually going to send that? Are you actually going to ask him if your dog is really a vampire?"

I sucked in a deep breath. "I have no idea what you're talking about."

"Come on, Jimmy. Everyone knows about your crazy theory. It's common knowledge." She snorted. "And PS—no offense, but it *is* kind of childish."

FACT: When people start a sentence with "No offense," they're about to say something really offensive.

I thought for a second. Irwin or Baxter must have mentioned my theory about Abby to Chad, and Chad told his brother Jared, and Jared told his girlfriend—who happens to be my sister, Misty.

I made a mental note to get mad at Irwin and Baxter and Chad later.

"So what?" I said to Misty. "I can write to Elroy Evans if I want, and you can't stop me."

Misty started playing with one of her curlers. "Of course I can't stop you, silly. And personally, I think it's great that you have a wild imagination."

I looked at her in shock. "You do?"

"Yup." Then she giggled. "As long as you realize that he's never, ever, ever, ever, EVER going to write you back. He's a famous author, and they don't have time for little kids with crazy theories."

"Says you," I said. "And I'm *not* a little kid!"

Misty smacked me on the arm. "Go right ahead, fanboy. If you're lucky, maybe his agent's assistant will send you a picture with a fake autograph from one of those machines." And she bounced out of the room, curlers and all.

"Forget you," I said, mostly to myself. Then I opened up the computer and finished my letter.

> PS Please write back so I can show my sister.

CHAPTER 7

T**HE** N**EXT** D**AY** was Saturday, which meant it was time for our weekly CrimeBiters meeting. We met at our head-quarters, on the roof-deck of the old abandoned Boathouse just off Nash's Swamp. No one ever went there except us—it was perfect.

At exactly thirteen minutes before two o'clock, Abby and I climbed the stairs to the roof. I was positive I'd be the first one there. I had a big announcement planned, and I wanted to mentally prepare.

Imagine my surprise when I saw Daisy already sitting there, reading a book.

We hadn't said or texted a word to each other since she'd walked into Isaac's store the day before.

"Oh, hey," I said.

She looked up at me but didn't smile. "Hey." She looked back down at her book.

I took Abby's leash off, and she went over to Daisy and

nuzzled her. Daisy nuzzled her back. My heart melted, of course.

"Where are the other guys?" Daisy asked, without taking her eyes off Abby.

"I'm not sure. I think Irwin is coming from his cello lesson. Don't know where Baxter is."

"Oh."

I sat down in an old lounge chair on the other side from where Daisy was sitting. I thought she might ask me why I was sitting so far away from her, but she didn't.

She read, and I sat, for what seemed like two hours, even though it was probably only two minutes.

"How's Purrkins?" I asked, after I couldn't take it anymore. Purrkins was Daisy's cat. She was really cute, and

even though she and Abby didn't get along at first, they were good friends now.

FACT: Relationships can be complicated. Between animals AND between humans.

"She's great," Daisy said. "As long as she's relaxing, looking out the window, or snoozing, she's a happy camper."

"Oh, cool." Cats are really different from dogs. They are perfectly happy doing nothing and staying indoors all the time. I didn't quite understand why some people loved them so much. But I wasn't about to say that out loud.

"Baxter and I are here!" hollered Irwin, from below.

They huffed and puffed their way up the stairs, saw me and Daisy sitting on opposite sides of the roof, and stopped in their tracks.

"What's going on?" Baxter asked.

"Nothing!" Daisy chirped cheerily. "We were just talking about how awesome pets are—they don't judge, they don't try to change you, they just love you for who you are."

Ouch.

"I agree," I said. "And they don't make you feel bad for what you believe in either."

"Whatever," Irwin said. "Do we have any CrimeBiters business to discuss? I can't stay long—my mom is taking me to Sal's so we can figure out what kind of pizza we want at the party."

"Wow, you'd think you were planning a mission to Mars or something," I said.

"Hardly," Irwin responded. "This is way more important."

Everyone laughed, which eased the tension a little bit. It seemed like as good a time as any to make my big announcement, so I stood up. "Well, actually, I have one important item on the agenda, and we might as well get straight to it." I paused for dramatic effect. "I have decided to step down as president of the CrimeBiters, effective immediately."

They all stared at me.

"It's true," I said. "I have been president ever since we started the club, and I think it's time for someone else to take over. In fact, I know just the person. I nominate Daisy Flowers for president."

Daisy looked at me like I had three heads. "Wait, what?"

"Whoa, whoa, whoa, hold on a second," Irwin said. He started rubbing his hands together, which is something he does when he is nervous. "We need to talk about this. I mean, I think it's really nice that you want to let someone else be president. I do."

"So, what, then?" I asked.

"Well, it's just that—" Irwin paused for a second. "I guess, well, I would also like to be considered for president."

D'oh, I thought to myself. *I hadn't thought of that.*

Irwin kept rubbing. "I mean, I was the second person to join the club, really, and I've been your friend the longest."

"I thought we all formed the club at the same time," I said.

"I nominate Irwin!" Daisy said. "He would be an awesome president."

Irwin smiled like he'd just won the gazillion-dollar lottery.

I looked at Baxter. "Do you want to be president too?"

He shook his head about ten times. "Absolutely not."

"Okay, then. We have two nominees for president." I hesitated, not sure what to say or do next.

Daisy looked up at me. "Why don't you want to be president anymore? I thought you were doing a good job."

I'd been thinking about it since the night before, when I wrote the letter to Elroy Evans. I'd been thinking about how Daisy had said the stuff about just seeing her as an object of fascination and not as an actual person. And how the best way to prove to them that I wasn't a little kid was to make a very mature, careful decision.

But I didn't really want to go into any of that stuff, so instead I said, "I just think it's time, that's all."

"Okay, then," said Baxter, who was always the most interested in getting on with things. "Like Jimmy said, we have two nominees. Which means we have to have an election."

D'oh, I thought to myself for the second time in two minutes.

"Good idea," I said. "All in favor of—"

"Hold on!" Baxter interrupted. "It needs to be a secret ballot, of course."

Triple d'oh.

"Jimmy, is everything okay?" Daisy asked. "You seem a little slow today."

"Yeah, no, I'm fine. Uh, how do we do a secret ballot? There's only four of us."

"You know what?" Irwin blurted. "You know what? Fine. Fine. I think Daisy being president is a good idea. I support Daisy too. All in favor of Daisy, say *aye*."

"Huh?" Baxter asked. "Why would we say *eye*?"

"Aye!" Irwin was losing his patience. "It's pronounced *eye*, but it's spelled A-Y-E! As in, yes!"

"I never heard that before," muttered Baxter. "But, uh . . . aye."

I raised my hand. "I aye too."

Irwin rolled his eyes (not his ayes). "You don't say it like that. You just say *aye*." Then he raised his hand. "The ayes have it. Congratulations, Daisy, you're the new president of the CrimeBiters."

Baxter, Irwin, and I clapped. Abby looked up at us sleepily, gave one thump of her tail, then went back to sleep.

"Speech!" proclaimed Baxter. "Speech!"

Daisy was blushing a little, but she was smiling from ear to ear. "I don't know what to say, you guys. This is a huge honor, and a big responsibility. I think Jimmy has done an amazing job leading the club so far, and I promise to continue his fine work and make you all proud." Everyone clapped again, and she walked over to Irwin.

"And as my first act as president, I would like to name Irwin Wonk as my vice-president."

It was Irwin's turn to grin widely. Baxter clapped and hooted. "Aye!" he hollered. "Aye! Aye!"

I froze.

Daisy squinted at me. "Jimmy?"

I wasn't sure what to say. This wasn't part of the plan. The plan was to make Daisy president so she would realize I was a thoughtful mature person and not be mad at me anymore. It wasn't to put Daisy and Irwin in charge of everything and leave me out in the cold.

But there wasn't a dang thing I could do about it at this point.

FACT: Sometimes, when you're feeling sorry for yourself, you do things for the wrong reasons.

ANOTHER FACT: Once you do those things, it can be very difficult to undo them.

"Oh, right, aye for sure," I said. "Congratulations to you both."

Daisy gave me a hug right then and there. "Awww, thanks, Jimmy. This is a really sweet thing you did, and I won't ever forget it."

I may have glowed with happiness for a minute there, but I can't quite remember, because it was overshadowed by what happened next.

"I want to bring something up," Daisy said. "It seems . . . and I don't want to act all like, *oh now I'm president, so I want to change everything* . . . but . . . I think we should think about changing where we meet."

My ears started to get hot. "Huh?" I said, because it was the only thing I could think of.

Daisy made a wide sweeping gesture with her hands. "It's just that . . . well, if you want to know the truth, I've always thought this old Boathouse was kind of gross. It's, like, really dirty and disgusting, and everything is broken. I think our club deserves a better clubhouse, that's all."

Irwin looked like he wasn't sure what to do, since he loved the Boathouse but had just been named the new vice-president by the new president, who apparently hated the Boathouse.

"Wait, really?" Baxter asked, which was pretty polite of him, if you ask me.

I was a lot less polite. "Are you serious? This is the greatest clubhouse ever! And it's all ours! Nobody even thinks about this place anymore—it's like our secret hideout!" I pointed at Abby, who was snoozing on her back. "Plus, Abby loves running around here, exploring the woods and the swamp and everything!"

"More like she *used* to," Irwin mumbled. "Now she pretty much naps all the time."

Daisy frowned. "Jeez, Jimmy, I didn't realize you felt so strongly. And I agree that it's important to keep our pets happy." She twirled her hair nervously. "That's actually one of the reasons I wanted to move the headquarters. I thought maybe we could try my house, at least for a little while. That way Purrkins could attend the meetings, since she is the other animal member of the CrimeBiters."

I stared at her in disbelief. Her house? Seriously? It was true, her cat, Purrkins, was a member of the club, but

I think the rest of us all assumed that was pretty much . . . how should I put it . . . *honorary.*

"Whatever!" I sat down in a huff. "I don't aye this one. I vote we keep our headquarters here."

"So that's one nay," Daisy said. "All the rest of us, if you're in favor of having the next meeting at my house, just to see how it feels, where ice-cream sandwiches and lemonade will be served, please raise your hand and say aye."

I turned toward the marshy swamp and stared off into the distance so I wouldn't have to watch my friends betray me. Because I knew that's exactly what they were going to do.

"Aye," I heard Baxter say. That didn't really surprise me, because he never really liked the Boathouse all that much. It was hard to blame him, considering his dad fell through the roof here and broke his back.

FACT: Read all about Mr. Bratford's Boathouse mishap and other crazy adventures in CRIMEBITERS! MY DOG IS BETTER THAN YOUR DOG. Act now, and you'll win a free toaster! (Not really.)

"What about you, Irwin?" Daisy asked.

There was a pause. Like I said, Irwin loved the Boathouse. He thought it was as cool as I did, because we used to come here all the time by ourselves and have a blast. It was our private clubhouse way before the CrimeBiters even existed.

I turned around and snuck a glance at Irwin. He saw me and quickly looked away.

"Will the lemonade be homemade?" I heard him ask.

I knew it was over right then and there.

"Oh yes!" Daisy exclaimed. "My mom makes the best lemonade ever."

"Okay, then," Irwin said nervously. "Aye."

Daisy clapped her hands. "Yay! I think this will be great!" Then she turned to me and added, "But afterward, if we decide we prefer the Boathouse, then we can always come back here. Fair enough?"

I wanted to say okay. I really did. I wanted to be sensible and respect the process and all that stuff. But for some reason, I just couldn't. This all started because I wanted to do something nice for Daisy, and then the next thing I knew, my club was being taken away from me, and there wasn't anything I could do about it.

So I didn't say okay. Instead, I said, "I think this stinks."

I know—not very presidential of me, right? Not even very ex-presidential.

Daisy's eyes suddenly turned cold. "I'm sorry you feel that way," she said. "I really am. But we voted, and the vote stands."

"Fine," I said. "Is the meeting over? Because I have to go."

I turned to leave, but something stopped me.

Or I should say, some*one* stopped me.

And it was the largest person I'd ever seen.

CHAPTER 8

"HELLO," SAID THE giant who'd interrupted our meeting. He was wearing a really cool uniform, with shiny black shoes and a red beret. It was like he appeared out of a dream. "Hope I'm not interrupting. I was told I'd find you guys here." His eyes locked on Baxter. "Hey, little buddy."

Baxter's eyes started getting wider and wider until I got worried that they were going to pop out of his head. He stood up slowly, staring at the giant. Finally, with his voice barely above a whisper, he said, "Bennett? Is that you?"

The man's face broke out in a huge grin. "It's me, dude. Live and in person."

Baxter jumped up like he'd been shot out of a cannon and ran into the man's arms, while the rest of us stared, openmouthed. *Holy moly.* This was Bennett, Baxter's brother? The one who had been in all sorts of trouble before joining the army? He looked like he'd stepped right off a movie screen.

PROFILE

Name: Bennett Bratford

Age: 22, but his uniform made him look 30

Occupation: Soldier

Interests: Defending our country

"Guys, this is my brother, Bennett," Baxter said, still seeming kind of shocked.

"That's awesome," Irwin said. "We didn't even hear you come upstairs, sir."

Bennett laughed. "No need to call me sir. And being quiet is one of the things they teach you in basic training." He looked down at his brother. "Turns out that before they ship you overseas, they let you go home for a few days to check in with the fam—so here I am."

"Did you see Mom yet?" Baxter asked.

"I sure did." Bennett took off his hat and scratched his head, which was bald, just like his brother's and father's (it was a family thing). "You should have seen her, Bax. She just about fainted right there in the kitchen."

Abby chose that moment to wake up, and she immediately started barking at the strange man who loomed over us.

"Abby!" I said, a little embarrassed. "This is Baxter's brother! He's in the army! Be nice!" Abby looked up at me and then piped down, luckily.

Irwin petted her and chuckled. "Where was that attitude when the guy outside Isaac's store almost knocked you over?"

"Ha-ha," I said sarcastically, even though I was thinking the same thing.

Daisy walked up to Bennett and stuck out her hand. "It's an honor to meet you, sir. Thank you for your service."

Bennett smiled and shook her hand. "You're welcome, but like I said, please don't call me sir. You can call me Private, and that's about it. What's your name?"

"Daisy," Daisy said shyly.

"Nice to see that Baxter has a lady friend," Bennett said. "I'm impressed."

Before that conversation went any further, Irwin and I rushed over and shook Bennett's hand too. "You're awesome," I said, kind of dumbly.

Bennett laughed. "Not really, but thanks," he said. Then he looked down at his brother. "Mom told me you'd be here. What is this, some kind of gang you guys are all in?" He looked around. "I love your clubhouse—it's super cool."

I smiled, and a warm glow spread throughout my body. "Some of us think so too," I said smugly.

"Jimmy and Irwin have been coming here for years," Baxter told his brother. "But we just had a vote and named Daisy president of the club, and we decided that we could use a change of scenery, so we're going to have the next meeting at her house and have ice-cream sandwiches and homemade lemonade."

When I heard Baxter put it that way, it all sounded so . . . I don't know . . . *reasonable.*

"Wow, that sounds super cool too," Private Bennett Bratford said. "A vote! Democracy at work! That's the American way, right? I love it."

Bennett picked up his little brother as easily as he would a small toy and threw him on his shoulders. "Let's go home, okay, Bax? There's some fried chicken in the fridge with my name on it."

"You bet!" Baxter waved at us. "See you guys later, okay?" And off they went.

Irwin, Daisy, and I all looked at one another. When you meet someone who is actually defending your country, and your right to vote, and your right to have a club that can meet wherever you want, there isn't really much left to say.

"I'm sorry if I was a jerk," I said to Daisy.

"And I'm sorry if I ambushed you with my idea to meet at my house," she said to me.

"And I'm sorry that I made fun of Abby not defending you at Isaac's," Irwin added.

"It's okay," we all said to each other.

And then we went home.

PART TWO

GOING APE

CHAPTER 9

A FEW DAYS a week, I volunteer at Shep's shelter. Shep's, which is run by this awesome guy named Shep Lansing, is the animal rescue place where I adopted Abby. But one of the most fun things about volunteering there is that I get to hang around with Kelsey Breed, the head animal trainer. Kelsey is from England, and I think she is really smart, although it's possible her accent might have something to do with it.

FACT: English accents make people sound really smart. And rich too. I have no idea why.

I don't think Kelsey was rich, but she *was* really smart, and she knew a lot about a ton of things. I liked just listening to her talk, because I always learned something.

FACT: I think people learn a lot more by living out in the world than they do by going to school. Don't tell my parents I said that. And especially don't tell *your* parents I said that.

The day after our meeting at the Boathouse, while I was on break and Kelsey was doing paperwork, I started telling her about Bennett Bratford, and how impressive he was, and how we were all so excited to be in his presence.

"I do love a man in uniform," Kelsey said, with a dreamy look in her eyes. "Especially an army man." She looked at me. "Did you know that even though Great Britain and the United States fought against each other in your war for independence, we have since become each other's greatest military allies?"

"Wow," I said, which was my way of saying, *To be honest, I most certainly did not know that.*

"It's quite true." Kelsey put her pen down and rubbed her eyes. "Well, that's it. Seventeen adoptions this week, Jimmy. Not bad. Not bad at all." She eyed the book in my hand. "What's that you've got there?"

I looked at the cover. "Oh, this? It's called *Fangs for Everything,* by Elroy Evans. He writes great mysteries about this really cool vampire named Jonah Forrester. They've been my favorite books since, like, forever."

Kelsey picked it up and looked at the cover. "Cool. Are you into vampires?"

"A little, I guess." *Understatement of the century.*

"Me too," she said. "I should check this guy out." She put the book down. "Want to hear something wild? Some people think Prince Charles—the son of our current Queen Elizabeth—is a direct descendant of the real Count Dracula."

"No way," I said, even though I wasn't completely sure who Prince Charles was—or Queen Elizabeth, for that matter. But I definitely knew who Count Dracula was. "That is so cool."

"Oh, there's a lot of fascinating stuff about vampires out there," Kelsey said. She stood up. "Well, I've got a beagle to train. Apparently he finds laptops delicious. Need to disabuse him of that notion. Ta-ta, Jimmy."

But I had a question for Kelsey now that I knew she was a vampire expert. "Hey, can I ask you something? Have you ever heard about a vampire losing their powers? Does that ever happen?"

Kelsey considered that for a second. "Well, I suppose it can. I mean, I'm sure in the long history of vampires, there must have been one or two who just stopped being vampires somewhere along the way, right?"

"Yeah, probably," I agreed.

"Why do you ask?"

I thought for a second, then decided to just go on to my next question. "And do vampires have to be human? I mean, do you think it's possible for other kinds of species to be vampires?"

Kelsey looked at me with an odd expression on her face. "Uh, like what kind of species? Do you know a giraffe who's a vampire or something?"

I looked over at Abby, who was sweetly playing with a squeaky toy that looked like a mouse. I knew I was in a tricky spot. If I told Kelsey that I thought Abby was a vampire but now I wasn't sure, she would definitely think I was insane. And once you think someone is insane, it's really hard to unthink it.

"Oh, not really," I said. "I just like to think about stuff like that sometimes. I guess I have kind of a weird imagination."

"Well, to answer your question, I think none of us really knows the truth about vampires," Kelsey said. She looked around the shelter as if she were worried someone might think *she* was insane. "That's what makes them so fascinating. The great unknown. So, yes—I do think it's possible that other species can be vampires. And you know what? I think it would be *awesome*."

Kelsey gave me a smile and walked away. I picked up

my book and tried to read, but I was too relieved to concentrate.

If the possibility of a vampire dog was good enough for a smart grown-up person from England, then it was good enough for me.

"Fangs for everything," I told Abby.

She thumped her tail and went back to her mouse.

CHAPTER 10

THINGS HAD SURE changed at school lunch.

It's hard to believe, but about a year ago Irwin and I used to sit at a corner table in the back of the cafeteria near the vending machines. Sometimes we would pretend to be judges on a TV reality show, making comments about this person's clothes, or that person's glasses, but what we were really doing was trying to ignore the fact that we didn't have any other friends. Then, after Daisy, Baxter, Irwin, and I formed the CrimeBiters, we moved more to the center of the room, where we discussed club business as if the future of the world depended on it—and, as far as we were concerned, it did.

Then I started playing lacrosse, and I became friends with Chad and the other guys on the team. For a while, I would alternate sitting with the CrimeBiters and the athletic kids. But all that did was kind of annoy everybody—especially me, because I had to listen to Irwin say things like, "What do you guys talk about at that table—stupid sports stuff?" Finally one day I walked over to the CrimeBiters table and told them to join me at the lacrosse table. "Sit over here with us. It won't kill you," I said, and they all looked at me like it would, in fact, kill them. "Come on," I pleaded, and then Daisy got up, and then Baxter got up too, and eventually even Irwin got up, and they followed me over to the lacrosse table and sat down, and the world didn't end, and we all actually had fun together. After that, we started sitting together all the time.

Like I said, things sure had changed.

So there I was, on the Monday after the whole cheerleader–president of CrimeBiters–Baxter's brother weekend, sitting and having lunch with Chad and two other guys from the basketball team and Irwin and Baxter from the anything-but-basketball team.

"Thanks for coming to the game on Friday," Chad said to Irwin and me. "That was pretty cool. You guys didn't have to do that."

"Oh, we wanted to," Irwin said, grinning from ear to ear. He was still getting used to the idea of the cool sports kids being nice to him, so he tended to smile extra widely around them. "And you played great."

Chad laughed self-consciously. "I was kind of off that game. My shot wasn't falling at all."

"Seriously?" I said. "I saw you make, like, seven great plays in five minutes."

"Aw, not really. But thanks."

It was kind of amazing how nice of a guy Chad was. I'm pretty sure if I was great at everything the way Chad is, I would not be nearly that nice.

Just then, Daisy came over with Mara, both carrying lunch trays. "Is there any way you can make room for us?" she said, even though she knew that of course we would. I made room for Daisy, but Mara ended up taking the seat, while Daisy plopped down next to Chad.

Hmmmm, I thought to myself.

"What's everybody talking about?" asked Mara. "Anything good?"

Baxter had a mouth full of french fries, but that didn't stop him from answering. "Chad was telling us how he thought he didn't play very well in the basketball game the other day, even though Irwin and Jimmy thought he played amazing. I have no opinion, because they didn't invite me to go with them."

"Really?" Daisy said. "That's not very nice, you guys."

I glared at Baxter. "You hate basketball."

"So do you," he said back, and he wasn't wrong. I looked at Daisy. "You texted Irwin to come down to the game. You didn't text Baxter or me. So it's really your fault."

It was Daisy's turn to glare. "I wrote that you should *all* come."

"This is a dumb argument," Irwin said, and he wasn't wrong either. "Can we talk about something else?"

"I agree with Irwin," Chad said, which made Irwin grin like a five-year-old at a fudge factory. Chad turned to Daisy. "You were great at cheerleading," he said. "I had no idea you could do flips like that. That halftime show was pretty cool." Then he looked at Mara, to make sure she didn't feel left out. "You were great too."

"Thanks!" Mara chirped. "I love to cheer!" Yeah, no kidding.

Daisy smiled shyly in Chad's direction. "It was my first time, and I was really nervous. Hopefully I'll get better."

"Are you kidding?" Chad exclaimed. "You were awesome." He leaned over in my direction. "My dad told me the reason I didn't play very well is because I was distracted by Daisy and the rest of the cheerleaders. He said I was watching them when I was supposed to be guarding my man."

Irwin laughed as if Chad had just told the funniest joke ever created by humans. But I wasn't laughing. I was watching Daisy, who was pretending not to listen but whose face was slowly turning deep red.

"If I didn't know any better," Baxter said, observing the whole thing, "I'd say that Chad and Daisy were flirting."

Daisy looked horribly offended. "That's ridiculous!" But I could tell by her face that it wasn't ridiculous at all—in fact, it was the opposite of ridiculous. It was true.

I suddenly got that weird feeling again—the same one I got when I first saw Daisy cheerleading. But this time, it was about a hundred times stronger. Because now I had proof, right in front of me.

Daisy liked a boy who wasn't me.

I suddenly had this feeling that I had to get away from there as quickly as possible. I stood up so abruptly that my chocolate milk fell over, spilling onto Baxter's tray. "Hey!" he protested.

"Sorry," I said. "But I just remembered I have to go do something. Plus, I'm not hungry." And without another word, I got up, whirled around, and left.

Or, I *would* have left, if Clarice hadn't been in my way.

Clarice, who runs the cafeteria at school, is the nicest person in the world. She does everything from make the pizza to refill the napkins in the napkin dispenser. At that exact moment, she was bringing a large tray of lasagna out from the kitchen.

Or, she *would* have brought the lasagna out from the kitchen, if I hadn't been in her way.

But as it turns out, we were *both* in each other's way. And so, we smashed right into each other, and her entire tray of lasagna went flying—all over her, and all over two tables full of kids.

The only one who escaped lasagna-free was me.

Immediately, kids started screaming things like "EW! GROSS!" and "ARE YOU KIDDING ME?" and "MY SHIRT IS RUINED!" I noticed that Chad was covered in tomato sauce, and Daisy was picking noodles out of her hair.

FACT: Lasagna is not a good look on a person.

"Oh my goodness!" Clarice exclaimed. "What a mess! I am so terribly sorry!" She immediately started trying to help all the kids who were doused in lasagna, but I just stood there, frozen. She looked up at me. "Jimmy? Are you okay?"

"This wasn't my fault," I said, which wasn't an answer to her question.

Ms. Owenby, my math teacher, was on lunch duty that day, and she came running over. "What happened here?"

"It wasn't my fault," I said again.

A few of the school custodians came over and started cleaning up the mess, and other teachers came over to get kids cleaned up. I made sure not to look at any of them. "Nobody said it was anyone's fault," Ms. Owenby said. "But you know you're not supposed to get up in the middle of lunch, right? And there's absolutely no running in the cafeteria, ever."

"I wasn't running. I was just—I had to go to the bathroom."

Ms. Owenby looked at me intently. "Honestly?"

I glanced up and saw Chad and Daisy whispering something to each other. Irwin and Baxter were standing next to them, and they looked like they were trying not to giggle. My ears started to burn, and the next thing I knew, I blurted out, "I don't care if you believe me or not! And besides, Clarice shouldn't have been walking behind me like that! Forget all you guys!" I could feel tears start to form behind my eyes, and I prayed they wouldn't start to leak out.

Ms. Owenby stared down at me. "I'm quite sure that blaming Clarice is not the solution here, young man. I think it might be a good idea if you went to Mr. Klondike's office to cool off for a little while."

I blinked at her. "Mr. Klondike's office?"

"Indeed."

I noticed I was breathing hard and tried to make myself calm down. Mr. Klondike is our vice-principal, in charge of misbehaving students. I actually get along with him pretty well, ever since we discovered we both had rescue dogs, but still—his office wasn't a place you wanted to visit, if you could help it.

"Okay," I muttered.

"Do I need to walk you down there, or can I trust you to go by yourself?"

"I can do it."

As I walked slowly out of the cafeteria, I could sense someone coming up behind me, and then I felt a hand on my arm.

I turned to see Daisy standing there. She still had a few noodles in her hair, but she didn't seem to care about that.

"Are you okay?" she asked me.

"Oh yeah," I said. "I'm fantastic."

And then I went to find out how much trouble I was in.

CHAPTER 11

WHEN YOU'RE SITTING outside Mr. Klondike's office, the first thing you see is a giant poster of a kitten sitting in a bathtub filled with milk. The slogan reads, SOMETIMES ENOUGH IS ENOUGH.

I waited there for a few minutes, staring at that kitten, until his assistant, Mrs. Crowley, said, "You can go ahead in, hon."

"Thank you, Mrs. Crowley," I said, extra politely, since I was pretty sure Mr. Klondike could hear me.

I walked into his office, but Mr. Klondike was busy writing something, and he didn't look up.

"Jimmy," he said. "How very nice to see you as always. Take a seat."

I did as I was told, then waited for about three minutes as Mr. Klondike finished what he was doing.

FACT: When you're sitting in the vice-principal's office, three minutes feels like three hundred and thirty-three minutes.

Finally he lifted his head. "Do you want to tell me what happened?"

"Clarice and I bumped into each other, and the lasagna spilled," I mumbled.

"I see." Mr. Klondike put his pen down. "That sounds like an unfortunate accident. But from what I understand, you then decided to blame everyone except yourself. Including Clarice, who may be the most beloved employee at the entire school."

The way he described it, it sounded like I'd acted like a total jerk.

Which was the moment I realized that I *had* acted like a total jerk.

"I—It was—"

Mr. Klondike waved his hand at me. "I'm not interested in your explanation, only your apology, which you should offer to all those involved."

I hung my head. "I will."

"Good. Then that's settled." I waited for Mr. Klondike to either punish or dismiss me, but instead he got up and looked out his window for a second. Then he turned around and sat down in the chair next to me. "Jimmy, I've known you for a while now, and I've always thought of you as one of our most mature students."

You're the only one, I thought to myself.

"This kind of behavior seems completely out of character for you," Mr. Klondike went on. "So maybe you can tell me what this is really about. Is there something else going on?"

"No," I said, without thinking about it. "Everything's fine."

"Okay, then. You can go."

I stared up at him. "Really? I'm not in trouble?"

"No, you're not in trouble, as long as you make sure to apologize."

"I will; I promise." I grabbed my backpack, leaped up,

and headed to the door. But then I stopped and turned back. At first, I wasn't even sure why.

"Mr. Klondike?" I asked.

He was already writing again, but he stopped and looked up. "Yes, Jimmy?"

I took a breath. "You know how sometimes you can really believe something? And you've believed in it for a long time, even though it's usually, like . . . well . . . something that maybe only a little kid would believe in?"

"You mean like Santa Claus?"

"Kind of, I guess, yeah." I took another step back into his office. "Like, the thing is, everyone thinks you're crazy for believing it, but still, deep down, you're convinced it's true, you know? Until one day you realize that maybe all those people might have been right all along, and you were wrong? Has that ever happened to you?"

"I'm not sure that it has, Jimmy, but I can imagine that it's not a great feeling."

"Yeah, it's not."

"Do you want to tell me what it is that you're talking about?"

I thought for a second and then shook my head. "Not right now if it's okay. Maybe someday though."

Mr. Klondike took his glasses off for a second and rubbed his eyes. "The only thing I can tell you, Jimmy, is you need to give yourself every chance to prove that you are right. Do your homework, do your research, and I promise you will be satisfied. Possibly not with what you discover, but with the fact that you did everything possible to know the truth, one way or the other. That's why knowledge is so important in this world."

"Thank you, Mr. Klondike. I will."

"Please say hello to Abby for me," he said. For a second I thought he knew exactly what I was talking about, but then I realized he was just being friendly.

FACT: Having a nice vice-principal is something that takes getting used to.

CHAPTER 12

THE FIRST THING I did when I got home after school on Monday was google "how to tell if your dog is a vampire."

It's very possible that I was the first person in history to do that.

But you know what the amazing thing about Google is? In .46 seconds, there were 2,580,000 results. Of course, most of the results had nothing to do with finding out if your dog is a vampire. Most of them were jokes, or vampire chat rooms, or websites that tried to sell you weird stuff like pills that help you grow fangs. (Do they really work?) I was about to give up when I saw one result that caught my eye. *VAMPIRE DOG TEST*, it said. *IS YOUR DOG A VAMPIRE DOG?*

I clicked on it.

Your dog has huge fangs, it said. *She's wide awake at night and might even have a bit of a biting problem.*

I couldn't believe what I was reading. *Yes, yes, and yes,* I said to myself.

So naturally you're asking yourself: Is it possible my dog is a vampire? Well, guess what? You're not crazy.

I'm not crazy! I said to myself. *You hear that, world? I'm not crazy!* But of course the world couldn't hear me, because I was talking to myself.

Well, you've come to the right place! Just click here to discover the easy test that can help you find out once and for all: IS YOUR DOG A VAMPIRE?

Yessssssssssssss!

I clicked.

THE WORLD'S FIRST DOG VAMPIRE TEST—JUST $49.99! We accept all major credit cards and PayPal.

Noooooooooooo!

I started clicking like a madman, trying to figure out a way to get the test without having to pay for it, when I heard the front door open and close. "Jimmy?" called my dad. "Are you home? What are you up to?"

I was running out of time, but I wasn't about to give up. There had to be a way in! I needed to get this test! My reputation depended on it! It was the most important thing I'd ever—

There was a knock on my door. "Hey, buddy, there you are. Whatcha doin'?"

I slammed the computer shut. "Oh, hey, Dad. Just looking up last night's Knicks score."

What, you thought I was going to tell my dad the truth? Ha!

"Oh, they lost, as usual," he said. "Being a Knicks fan is no fun these days, that's for sure."

"Yeah," I said, my fingers itching to get back to my online mission.

"Well, let's go," said my dad.

"Huh?"

"We need to get Irwin a present, remember? The party is tomorrow."

I slapped my forehead, just like you see in cartoons.

"Oh yeah!" I quickly considered my options, then realized I didn't have any. "Okay, great. Can we stop by The Super Scooper? I'm starving and I never had my after-school snack." The Super Scooper was my go-to treat spot before Isaac's came along. Now it's pretty much fifty-fifty.

"Hmmm, we'll see," said my dad, but he was winking when he said it.

I shot to my feet, the vampire test all but forgotten. "Cool! I'll be ready in two minutes."

Never underestimate the power of ice cream.

CHAPTER 13

LATER THAT NIGHT, I walked into the family room.

"Mom, Dad? Can I borrow fifty dollars?"

FACT: The best time to ask your parents for money is after a long day when they're relaxing on the couch and watching their favorite TV show.

"Absolutely not," my mom said.

CLARIFICATION: I said it was the BEST time to ask, not a GOOD time to ask.

"Please? I'll pay you back, I swear!"

My dad put the show on pause. "What on earth could you possibly need fifty dollars for?"

Well, I knew one thing. I wasn't going to say, "For a vampire dog test." So instead I said, "I want to get Irwin another present." Which didn't make a lot of sense, since we'd gotten him a really nice telescope.

My parents looked at each other. "Well, that's very thoughtful," said my mom. "But I think one present is quite enough, even for your best friend."

"Okay, great," I said, even though what I meant was, *That's not great at all.*

I went back to the kitchen, where Abby was hanging out on her favorite chair. She liked to chill out in the kitchen, in case anyone stopped by for a snack. She saw me coming and gave her tail a thump.

"Hungry, Ab?"

Another few whacks of the tail, harder this time.

As I looked at her, her tail wagging and her eyes bright with the hope of a treat, I had an idea. So what if I couldn't afford the online test? I could make up my own test!

"Mom! Do we have any garlic powder?"

"Huh?"

"The garlic powder! Where is it?"

"What the heck do you need the garlic powder for?"

"I just do!"

There was a brief pause, during which she must have decided that telling me where to find the garlic powder was less dangerous than lending me fifty dollars.

"In the cabinet to the right of the stove."

"Thanks!"

I opened the fridge and got out a few pieces of sliced turkey, which was Abby's favorite. Then I took some garlic powder and sprinkled it on top of the turkey. As I was preparing the experimental snack, I thought back to the first time Abby came across garlic, when Mrs. Cragg made me eat garlic muffins for breakfast. Poor Abby couldn't sprint out of the kitchen fast enough.

"How do you feel about garlic, Abby?" I asked. She cocked her head at me but refused to answer (dogs are like that). "Like all vampires, you're against it, right? I really hope you're against it."

As I put the extra turkey away, I called out, "Delicious treat!" which was her cue to jump out of the chair and start salivating and licking her lips.

Then I paused, thought a few good thoughts, and placed the snack on the ground.

Abby waited, just the way she was trained.

"Okay, go!" I announced.

She scampered over to the garlic turkey and gobbled it down in about zero seconds flat.

Then she looked up at me and asked for more.

My heart started to pound as I sat down at the kitchen table. I'd given Abby my homemade vampire dog test,

and she'd failed miserably! It was time to face the facts: Abby was looking less and less like a vampire.

It was very possible she was just a dog with big fangs who liked to stay up late.

"Okay, Abby," I said. "Even if you're not a vampire—and I'm not saying you're not, I'm just saying it's possible you're not—it doesn't matter. I still love you, and you're still the greatest dog in the world."

She looked up at me, thumped her tail once, lay down under the table, and was snoring in about five seconds flat.

Abby definitely wasn't losing any sleep over it, that's for sure.

CHAPTER 14

THE VERY FIRST birthday party I ever went to was my cousin Eddy's. I think he was turning five, and the party consisted of him, me, a girl named Melinda who had a habit of picking her nose and wiping it on her arm, and Eddy's neighbor Norman, whose laugh sounded like a hyena battling stomach problems. We played a few games, ran around outside under a sprinkler for a while, and then had a piece of vanilla cake with vanilla icing. (I hate vanilla.) It was lame, quiet, and over in about forty-five minutes.

Boy, times have sure changed.

As I walked down the street toward Irwin's party, I could already hear music blasting and see a big yellow jumping tent in his front yard. There were about fifty balloons strung around the front yard—I guess his decision on which colors to go with ended up being "all of them." In the driveway, there was a giant purple trailer that said AMAZING ANDY AND HIS AWESOME ANIMALS! on the side, with a painting of a jungle covering the whole thing.

Mrs. Cragg, my babysitter, was with me, holding Abby on a leash. "Holy cannoli," she said, whatever that meant. "This is some shindig."

We walked up to the side of the trailer, and Abby's tail shot straight up into the air as she caught a whiff of something wild. She started barking, and I immediately got excited that maybe she was showing some of her old spunk, but then I remembered that animals always get excited when they smell other animals.

Mrs. Cragg was struggling to control the leash as Abby kept lunging toward the trailer. "We better head back to the house before she breaks my arm."

I bent down and gave Abby a kiss on the top of her head. "See you guys in a few hours." Abby gave me a wag, Mrs. Cragg gave me a wave, and off they went. My babysitter and my dog, who used to be archenemies, were now great pals. Who woulda thunk it?

FACT: Of all the wacky CrimeBiters stories, there might be none wackier than the story of Agnes Cragg. If you don't believe me, look it up!

I went inside, and the first thing I saw was Irwin and Baxter, holding cupcakes, with frosting smeared over most of their faces. I was worried that they might still be mad from The Lasagna Incident (that sounds like a book title, doesn't it?), but as soon as they saw me they came racing over.

"Isaac made special peanut butter frosting just for me!" Irwin exclaimed. "It's the best thing I've ever tasted ever!"

"I think it's weird," Baxter said, but it didn't stop him from polishing off his last bite.

Irwin pointed at the present I was holding. "Wow, that's big."

"I know, right?" I knew he'd be excited by the telescope because he loved stars, and I was dying for him to open it. But he led me out to the screen porch, where all the presents were sitting on a table. I put my box down as Irwin looked lovingly at his loot. "I'm gonna open all these later, after Amazing Andy's show. Do you want to go outside and jump in the tent, or try the Slip 'N Slide, or have some food, or swim in the pool?" Baxter and I looked at each other, trying to decide. Irwin tapped his foot impatiently. "Or we could go watch Andy set up. He starts in ten minutes."

I looked around, trying to find Daisy, even though part of me didn't want to see her. But there she was, with Mara and another friend named Becky. They were eating pretzels and drinking soda and laughing. Chad was nowhere in sight, which I silently decided was a small victory.

"Can we check out the animals?" I asked. Irwin nodded excitedly. "Sure!" The three of us headed out to the backyard, which had been turned into a miniature zoo. There were cages all over the place—I saw birds, snakes,

turtles, a possum, a fawn, what looked like a small fox, and three baby raccoons. There were also more cages off to the sides, with blankets over them so I couldn't tell what animals were inside.

"Holy cannoli," I said.

"What does that mean?" Baxter asked.

I shrugged. "I have no idea."

At the far end of the yard, two men were busy setting up a stage with chairs and hoops and toys. They were both wearing bright-orange jackets that said AMAZING ANDY'S AWESOME ANIMALS! on them.

"Is one of those guys Amazing Andy?" I whispered to Irwin.

"Yup," he whispered back. "The tall one with the beard. The other guy is Reptile Ron, his assistant."

They saw us and waved. We waved back. "Can't wait to see the show!" I called.

Amazing Andy gave us a thumbs-up. "Can't wait for you to see it!"

Irwin turned to us. "Should we grab some lunch?" He didn't have to ask us twice. We hustled over to the food area, where Irwin's dad was grilling like a madman. "What can I get you boys?" he asked.

"Cheeseburgers, thanks!" announced Irwin and Baxter.

"I'd love a hot dog, please," I said.

Mr. Wonk threw a dog on the fire. "The burgers are ready now, but the hot dog will take just a minute." As Mr. Wonk went about his business, I noticed Chad playing Nerf football in the pool.

PROFILE

Name: Amazing Andy
Age: Younger than my parents, older than my sister
Occupation: Professional birthday party entertainer
Interests: Animals, of course

PROFILE

Name: Reptile Ron

Age: Old enough to hold a boa constrictor without being scared

Occupation: Professional birthday party entertainer's assistant

Interests: Animals with scales

I thought about joining him and the other sports guys, but then remembered I was a pretty lousy swimmer and a terrible football player. I saw Daisy still talking to her friends, and I didn't want to bother them either. Baxter and Irwin were busy chomping on their burgers, and other kids surrounded them, pounding on Irwin's back and wishing him a happy birthday. They all drifted away, totally forgetting that I was still waiting for my hot dog. Ordinarily I might not have noticed or cared, but after everything that had been going on lately, it was hard not to feel a little bit left out.

"Here ya go!" said Mr. Wonk, handing me a delicious-looking hot dog. It was dripping with grease and drenched in ketchup, just the way I liked it.

The only problem was I didn't have anyone to eat with.

CHAPTER 15

"WELCOME TO AMAZING Andy's Awesome Animal Show!"

Thirty kids roared as Amazing Andy leaped up onto the stage.

"This is my colleague and associate, Reptile Ron, and together we are going to introduce you to the mysterious, magical world of animals!"

Everyone went nuts again.

In the next thirty minutes, the following things happened:

A raccoon ate a stick of bamboo.

A snake curled around Irwin's stomach.

A fox ran up to the porch, used his teeth to grab a balloon by the string, ran back to Amazing Andy, and wrapped it around his foot.

A turtle climbed onto another turtle's back, and then they piggybacked across a table.

Two gophers played Ping-Pong with tiny rackets.

Irwin fed lettuce to a very small alligator. (I guess the alligator was in a bad mood though, because Reptile Ron had to leave in the middle of the show to return him to their trailer.)

An iguana named Leo sat on Baxter's head and peed.

And a bunch more stuff happened too.

I bet it was the greatest half hour of Irwin's life. If not, it was definitely in his top five. Everyone else loved it too. Mr. and Mrs. Wonk were grinning as if they were the greatest parents in the world—which at that very moment, I guess they were.

"And now," proclaimed Amazing Andy, "for our final exhibit of the afternoon, may I present to you Alfie, our beloved parrot, who has a special song prepared."

And with that, Reptile Ron whipped off a sheet that was covering a cage to reveal the biggest, most colorful bird I've ever seen. And you could tell this was a bird who loved performing in front of an audience. He took one look around, extended his wings as far as they would go and, believe it or not, took a long bow. I swear.

Then Alfie started to sing.

"Happy birthday to youuuuuuuuuu.

Happy birthday to youuuuuuuuuu.

"Happy birthday dear person whose birthday it is . . ."

He paused while Amazing Andy pointed to the crowd. We all yelled "IRWIN!!!!"

Alfie continued:

"Happy birthdaaaaaay toooooooooooo youuuuuuuuuuuu!"

The crowd was going nuts before Alfie finished his last note. Then he bowed again, even longer than last time.

"Thank you!" Andy yelled, while everyone cheered. "Thank you guys all so much! Have a great rest of your party! And happy birthday, Irwin!"

As all the kids started to chat excitedly about what they just saw, Mrs. Wonk held up her hand. "Hey, everyone, listen up. It's time for cake and presents!"

You could hear the "YAY!" all the way to the next town.

We all charged toward the screen porch. "No running!" Mrs. Wonk hollered, but she might as well have been trying to tell an ocean not to make waves. It was basically a stampede, led by her very own son, who was gleefully rubbing his hands together as he contemplated the joy of thirty presents just for him, followed by all the chocolate peanut-butter cake he could eat.

And then Irwin stopped short, which all the kids crash into him from behind. His mouth formed into the shape of a terrified scream, but no sound came out.

I ran up next to him. "Irwin? Are you okay? What is it?"

But before I could answer, Mrs. Wonk sprinted right by me, onto the porch. Her mouth also formed into the shape of a scream, but sound *did* come out. It sounded kind of like, "AAARRRRGHGHTEUWUWUWUFUUV UVSSSSTTTTTTEURGLE!"

Also, I think there might have been a curse word in there somewhere, but I can't quite be sure.

She lifted up a trembling arm and pointed. "The—the presents. They're gone. They're all gone."

My eyes shifted over to the table, where all the presents had been stacked up earlier like a tower of colorful delight. But now, there was nothing there. Not even a bow or a ribbon. All that was left was a plastic tablecloth, flapping in the breeze, with a small rip at one end.

"NOOOOOOOOO!" cried Irwin, who had found his voice. "MY PRESENTS!"

Mrs. Wonk yelled out, "Herbert! Herbert! Someone has stolen the presents!"

Herbert, who was Mr. Wonk, had gone back to the grill after the show. "What are you talking about?" he hollered back.

"SOMEONE HAS STOLEN THE PRESENTS!" screamed Mrs. Wonk.

"*MY* PRESENTS!" yelled Irwin, as if there were any confusion.

FACT: Animals don't like screaming and yelling.

While the various Wonks were trying to figure out how to deal with this horrible trauma, and the various kids were trying to figure out if this meant that we wouldn't be getting cake, there was a *SQUAWK!* from the stage, where Amazing Andy and Reptile Ron were still packing up the animals. We all turned just in time to see a skunk wiggle out of Andy's hands, sprint over to the porch area, turn around, and let out a blast of skunk spray in our direction.

"EWWWWW!" everyone screamed. People started running in every possible direction, trying to figure out if they got any skunk spray on them. All the noise made the little fox bounce up and down in his cage, the possum roll over and play dead, and Alfie the parrot proclaim, "HAPPY BIRTHDAY! HAPPY BIRTHDAY! HAPPY BIRTHDAY!" over and over in a nervous chatter.

By the time Irwin started crying, we *knew* we weren't getting any cake.

"Party's over!" announced Mrs. Wonk. "Everybody needs to call their parents!" I ran over to Irwin to try to make him feel better, but Baxter and Daisy had gotten to him first. Other kids were trying to cheer him up too, but we all knew it was a lost cause.

"Who would do that?" he kept saying, between sobs and gasps of air. "Who would take my presents?"

"I have no idea," I told him. "A terrible person, that's who."

Amazing Andy came up to the porch to find out what was going on. "Is everything okay? I heard a big commotion." He swung his head behind him. "Reptile Ron is trying to calm down the animals. They're all a bit spooked."

"No, Amazing Andy, everything is *not* okay," Mrs. Wonk said, with a tremble in her voice. "Somebody has ruined my son's perfect day by stealing all his birthday presents."

Andy's face turned white. "Oh no," he said. "Oh no, oh no, oh no. I'm so sorry."

"It's a disaster," Mrs. Wonk said.

Reptile Ron came running over. "I got everyone settled in," he said. "Rascal was a little tricky, but I managed to calm her down with some extra treats. What's going on?"

"The presents are gone," Andy said.

"Oh no," Reptile Ron said. "Not again."

Andy glared at him like he'd just told a secret.

"What do you mean?" asked Mr. Wonk.

Andy sighed and took a deep breath. "The same thing happened about a month ago, at another party we worked at," he said. "It was in Shoreview, a few towns over. We were in the cul-de-sac of a dead-end street, and all the presents had been put in one of the upstairs bedrooms. When we finished the show, everyone headed back to the house, and the presents were gone."

"That's crazy," Mr. Wonk said. "I think I should call the police."

Mrs. Wonk shook her head. "I don't want a whole thing right now with all these children around," she said. "We'll call later."

While everyone just stood there trying to figure out what to do next, a chirpy voice behind us said, "Does this mean you're not going to do *my* party?"

We all turned to see Mara standing there, her face bright red with excitement and worry. "Amazing Andy is performing at my party next Sunday," she explained. "I can't wait! You're still coming, right? You promised to bring a boa constrictor!"

"I did?" said Amazing Andy. "Oh, right, I did." He tried to smile reassuringly. "Of course I'll be there," he said.

"The show must go on. Everyone just needs to keep a closer eye on things, of course, so something like this never, ever happens again."

"Oh, we will!" Mara chirped. "We'll be super careful!"

I looked at Irwin, who was drying the last of his tears. "Did you hear that?" I said. "Amazing Andy is performing at Mara's party next week."

He nodded. "Yup, I heard. I hope the boa constrictor eats Mara's left arm."

Mr. and Mrs. Wonk looked appalled. "Irwin! That's a terrible thing to say!"

"Well, this has been a terrible day!" he yelled, and then he ran inside the house and slammed the door.

And that was the end of that.

FACT: There aren't many people angrier than a birthday boy whose party has just been ruined.

CHAPTER 16

SO IT TURNS out that ice-cream sandwiches and lemonade go really well together.

I wasn't about to admit it out loud though.

It was the Saturday after the Irwin party disaster, and the CrimeBiters had gathered for our first meeting at our new non-clubhouse, otherwise known as Daisy's TV room.

"Does everyone have enough to eat?" Daisy's mom sang out.

"Yes, thank you, Mrs. Flowers," we all tried to say through stuffed mouths.

"Very good." She left a big bowl of potato chips on the coffee table, just in case we weren't impressed enough with all the available refreshments.

"These go great with ice-cream sandwiches," mumbled Baxter, who proceeded to take a chip, scrape half the vanilla ice cream off the side of his ice-cream sandwich, and pop the whole thing in his mouth.

We all stared at him, until he managed to utter one more single word: "Yum."

"I call this CrimeBiters meeting to order!" announced Irwin. "The honorable Daisy Flowers, president, presiding!" He paused and scratched his head. "Hey, I wonder if *president* and *presiding* come from the same original word."

"Who cares?" I said. "And what's with the whole announcement thing? It's not like Daisy is the queen of England."

Irwin looked wounded. "I just thought we should treat the passing of the torch with some ceremony, that's all."

I glanced over at Baxter, but he was still working his potato chip–ice cream combination, so it was clear he was going to be no help. "Can we just get on with it?"

Daisy stood up. "Thank you, Irwin, for that wonderful introduction, although I do agree with Jimmy that we can be a lot more informal from now on."

If you really want to be informal, you can sit down while you talk, like I did, I thought to myself but didn't say out loud.

Daisy sat down, which made me wonder for a second if I *had* said that out loud. But then I decided that she just knew exactly what I was thinking at all times, which was more believable.

"Does anyone have any official club business they'd like to start with?" she asked.

Irwin raised his hand. "I'm not saying this just because I was the victim, but I think it's pretty obvious what our next case should be."

The rest of us looked at him, waiting.

"The birthday-party thief, of course! Somebody's out there ruining children's dreams, one birthday party at a time, and we need to stop them!"

Baxter cleared his throat, which was probably still full of salty, sugary goodness. "Uh, how are we supposed to do that? Get invited to every birthday party in the state and put secret cameras all over the houses?"

"Are you serious?" I asked.

"Of course not," Baxter answered.

"This is an extremely serious situation," Daisy said, very presidentially. "And a very tough case. Our first step should be to go to Mara's party tomorrow with our eyes and ears open, keep an eye on things, and see if something strange is going on. Then, afterward, we can formulate a plan for pursuing the case."

"That's going to take too long!" whined Irwin.

"You just want your presents back," I said—which, I have to admit, was a little mean-spirited. I guess I was having a hard time getting used to the not-president thing.

"Jimmy, please," Daisy said. "That's not helpful. Please keep your negative thoughts to yourself."

Ouch.

It was bad enough that they treated me like I was a little kid, but now Daisy was scolding me like I was a little brat.

"I think Daisy's idea is good," Baxter said. "And she's the boss, so what she says goes."

Double ouch.

Irwin and I looked at each other, wondering if we should object. But neither one of us was brave enough to challenge Madame President. Meanwhile, Mrs. Flowers came bustling back into the room, carrying another tray of delights.

"Yummy snacks for all!" she announced. "For my hardworking young crime fighters!"

"Wow, this is the best club meeting ever!" Baxter said.

Everyone grabbed a snack—even me, dang it. I bit into it, hoping it would be stale and terrible.

It was delicious.

THAT NIGHT, I lay in bed, tossing and turning, wondering where it had all gone wrong. Sure, maybe I was obsessed with vampires. Sure, maybe Abby wasn't a superhero crime-fighting vampire dog (although of course she was). And sure, maybe my friends were right that I needed to grow up. But all I knew was, I wasn't going to give up without a fight. I needed some way to prove them all wrong.

Then, in the middle of the night, I woke up with an idea.

I'll bring Abby to Mara's party, and she'll help me solve the case!

I smacked the pillow with excitement. It was simple; it was perfect; it was glorious.

Problem solved!

THE NEXT MORNING, as I buzzed around the house getting ready to go to the party, I put my plan into motion.

"Guess what?" I said to Mrs. Cragg. "Abby is invited to this party!"

"Is that right?" She was eyeing me skeptically. "Even with all those animals?"

"Yup. Look." I showed her the invitation I'd spent an hour creating before breakfast. (I woke up an hour early to do it.) (Hey, I was desperate.) *COME TO MARA'S WILD BIRTHDAY PARTY!* the invitation said at the top. *PETS WELCOME!* Then, to make it more believable, I'd added, *ALL PETS MUST LEAVE BEFORE THE PERFORMANCE.*

Mrs. Cragg examined the "invitation" as I watched

and waited. "Huh," she said, finally. "I must say I'm a bit surprised, but there you have it. Well, go leash up Abby and let's get going."

Yes! I started daydreaming . . . *This is my chance to prove them all wrong. The CrimeBiters will solve this case, and Abby will be a hero, just like in my dreams. Irwin and Daisy and—*

Oh, did I forget to mention that I hadn't told the other CrimeBiters about my plan to bring Abby to the party? Yeah, I knew they would think it was a terrible idea, and I just wasn't in the mood to hear all that negativity.

FACT: Sometimes people are negative for a good reason.

CHAPTER 17

MARA LIVED AT the end of a cul-de-sac called Red Robin Way.

FACT: Cul-de-sac is just a fancy way to say "dead end."

QUESTION: Why are there so many streets named after birds?

OPINION: I think it would have been better if it were named Wed Wobin Way.

When we drove up, Mrs. Cragg whistled. "Wow, pretty fancy neighborhood," she said. "I could have done some real damage here, back in the day." *Whoa.* That was the first time she'd ever mentioned her former life as a jewelry thief, except when she first starting working for our family and told us those were the darkest days of her life.

I stared over at her for a split second: Was there any possible way she was the birthday-present thief? Nah, couldn't be. Wait, could it?

She glanced over at me. "Oh, for goodness' sake, I didn't take those gifts, if that's what you're thinking," Mrs. Cragg said. "Not in a million years would I ever go back to such stupid behavior."

"Of course I wasn't thinking that."

Mrs. Cragg chuckled. "I'll bet you weren't."

"This is good," I said as she was about to turn into Mara's long driveway. "Abby and I can walk from here."

Mrs. Cragg looked surprised, but she stopped the car. "Really?"

"Yeah," I said, nodding. "Mara said to get dropped off here, because they didn't want people cluttering the driveway while the party was going on." I didn't want to tell her the real reason—you know, the part about no one knowing I was bringing Abby.

"Huh," muttered Mrs. Cragg. "Okay, hop out."

I grabbed Abby's leash, and we headed toward the house. After a few steps, we noticed Amazing Andy's big purple van at the exact same time. I kept going, but Abby stopped right in her tracks. Just like last time, the scent of the animals was just too fascinating for her doggy nose.

As I tried to pull her leash, I heard a noise from the other side of the van, and Amazing Andy and Reptile Ron popped their heads around.

"Hello there," Amazing Andy said. "Are you here for the party?"

I nodded. "Yup. I saw your show at Irwin's party, and it was amazing. Too bad the only thing people remember is that someone stole the presents."

Andy looked concerned. "Yeah, did they ever get to the bottom of that?"

"Nope," I told him.

Reptile Ron walked over. "This is a bit of a wrinkle," he said, scratching Abby. "Who said you could bring a dog?"

I tried to laugh it off. "Oh, you mean Abby? Everyone knows her. She's welcome everywhere."

Andy and Ron weren't laughing though. "Well, just make sure she stays far away from the stage when Bosco performs," Andy said.

"Who's Bosco?" I asked.

"He's our baby chimpanzee," Ron answered. "He's got a bit of an attitude when it comes to dogs."

I scratched my head. "Huh. Was Bosco at the last party? I don't remember him."

"Nope," Andy said. "He just finished training. This is his coming-out party." Andy pointed down at Abby, and his face got serious. "So like I said, please be sure to keep this cute little girl far away from the stage at that point. Maybe even keep her in the house."

"Oh, of course," I said. "Come on, Ab, let's go say hi to the guys." Abby, who was staring up at Reptile Ron, didn't look like she wanted to go anywhere, but after a few tugs on the leash, I finally got her to move. "Can't wait for the show," I said to Andy and Ron, and they waved.

As I walked toward the house, I started having second thoughts about bringing Abby. This whole Bosco thing was a surprise, but I decided as long as I kept Abby inside near where the presents were, it wouldn't be a problem.

As I was trying to decide whether to ring the front doorbell or scrap the whole thing, two girls tore around the side of the house, screaming with laughter. "Last one back to the party is a rotten egg!" one of them shouted. They were both completely soaking wet, so it took me a second to realize it was Daisy and Mara.

They stopped in their tracks when they saw me. Then they doubly stopped in their tracks when they saw Abby.

"Hi, you guys!" I said.

"Who?" said Mara, which didn't make any sense. She wasn't looking at me, she was looking at Abby, and her eyes were as big as saucers. Flying saucers. *Giant* flying saucers.

"What do you mean, who?" I asked, but Mara just stood there.

"Mara is really scared of dogs," Daisy said, by way of explanation.

"I was bitten by one when I was really little," Mara said, her voice barely above a whisper. "The dog who bit me looked like your dog." She backed up about five steps, never taking her eyes off Abby. Abby looked up at her and wagged her tail, but it didn't seem to help.

My heart sank. "Wow, really? That stinks. Abby is super friendly. She loves everybody."

"That's not quite true," Daisy said unhelpfully. "What were you thinking, bringing her here?"

"Well, now, that's a very good question," I said. "A really good question. One of your best questions ever."

Daisy eyed me. "So what's the answer?"

I leaned in and whispered so Mara wouldn't hear, "Well, to be honest, I thought she could help solve the Case of the Missing Presents."

"Are you serious?" Daisy said. The look on her face was a combination of displeasure and disbelief.

"What are you guys doing?" I asked, changing the subject. "Why are you running around the house?"

"Mara challenged me to a race. We love running against each other. We have to run three laps every day before cheerleading practice, because *cheerleading* is a *sport*."

"It sure is," I agreed, relieved that she wasn't yelling at me anymore about bringing Abby to the party. Then, hoping to score a few additional brownie points, I added, "I was really impressed with how good you guys were at cheering the other day."

"Thanks," Daisy said. "You need to take Abby home now."

Well, you can't blame a guy for trying.

"No problem," I said. "Sorry if it was any bother."

Daisy narrowed her eyes at me. "It wasn't yet, luckily for you." She turned to Mara. "We should probably get back to the party, since you're the guest of honor and people are going to start to wonder where you are."

Just then, the door to Amazing Andy's trailer opened, and there was Andy, holding the hand of a very small, very dark, very furry person. They started walking toward us, and I noticed the dark furry person had a funny way of walking. Then I noticed that it wasn't a person at all. It was a chimpanzee.

Andy was talking on his cell phone, so he didn't notice us at first. The little chimp noticed us right away though, and froze.

"How cute!" Mara squealed, which made me realize, if you *really* want to change the subject, a chimp will do the trick. "What's his name?"

"Uh-oh," I said. "That must be Bosco."

"Huh?" Daisy said.

"How do you know his name?" Mara said.

Before I could answer, Andy, who'd spotted us at last, called across the driveway, "Hey, wait a second. I thought I told you to do something with that dog!"

"I didn't realize you were coming out yet!" I yelled.

"I'm taking Bosco for a pre-show walk to calm his nerves!" he yelled back. "He tends to get very stressed out, and seeing your dog isn't helping!"

As if to prove Andy's point, Abby started barking at Bosco. Her bark got louder, and her fangs came out.

Oh great, I thought. *You know I love seeing your fangs, but now isn't exactly the best time.*

Bosco stood up to his full height—which wasn't very tall at all—and let out what he thought was a growl, but sounded more like an adorable squeak. To Abby though it was threatening enough, and she responded with a howl that made Mara scream and grab my hand. The problem was, it was the hand that was holding Abby's leash—which I promptly dropped.

Uh-oh.

Newly freed, Abby took off toward the terrified baby chimp, who got one look at the charging dog and took off herself. The next thing we knew, the two animals were tearing around the corner and going full speed toward the back of Mara's house.

"STOP THAT CHIMP!" hollered Andy. He sprinted after Bosco, with the rest of us right behind him.

When we turned the corner, I saw that the party was just getting going. Some kids were jumping through the sprinkler, and other kids were playing some sort of game that involved throwing popcorn and grapes into one another's mouths. Meanwhile, Mara's mom was setting up lunch at two long picnic benches, with small red and white balloons at every chair and a giant pink one tied to the glass at the head of the table—that must have been Mara's spot.

Everybody pretty much saw Bosco and Abby at the same time, and everything stopped.

"Is that a monkey?" someone asked.

"Is that Abby?" Irwin asked.

They were both right (although technically, Bosco was an ape).

Bosco and Abby's first stop was the drinks table, where a couple of kids had just finished pouring themselves glasses of root beer. Sadly, they didn't even get to take one sip before their drinks—and, in fact, every last bottle of soda and juice—were knocked over when the two animals crashed into the table.

"Hey!" said one of the kids.

"Where can we get more root beer?" said the other.

From there, Bosco and Abby headed over toward the picnic area, where Mrs. Lloyd was busy folding special BIRTHDAY FEAST! napkins.

"What the—?" she said, but she didn't get to finish her sentence, because Bosco dove onto the table headfirst and slid all the way down the middle, knocking over every plate, cup, hot dog, hamburger, potato chip, and cheese doodle. Abby didn't go up onto the table though— her move was to jump from chair to chair, bursting every balloon with her claws as she went by—*POP! POP! POP! POP! POP!* You get the idea.

Mrs. Lloyd stared dumbfounded for about fifteen seconds, and then screamed, "LLOYD!" No one could understand why she was shouting her own last name, until a man came out of the house and asked in a very mild-mannered voice, "What is it, dear?" It turned out that her husband's first name was Lloyd. As in, Lloyd Lloyd. I briefly wondered what kind of parents would do that to a child, but my attention immediately returned to Bosco and Abby, who had moved on to Amazing Andy's

stage. It was filled with pillows, because one of the first things Andy does is set up a pillow fight between the guest of honor/birthday boy or girl and an adorable raccoon named Roger. But unfortunately that pillow fight wasn't going to happen at this party, because Bosco found the cutest, softest, furriest pillow he could find—and pooped right on top of it.

"EWWWWWWW!" yelled pretty much everybody. Even Abby looked a little shocked.

But Bosco wasn't done. Absolutely not. No chance.

Not in a million years. Nope. After finishing his business, Bosco leaned over, admired his handiwork, then picked up a fairly sizable piece of his poop and threw it randomly over his shoulder in the general direction of the house, where it happened to land, with a gentle plop, just above Lloyd Lloyd's left ear.

Well, Lloyd Lloyd wasn't mild-mannered after that.

He made a noise that sounded kind of like "AIEUWHRHFHFHEIWWI-WIIIEEEGGGGH!" Then he ran over to the sprinkler and jumped into it head-first, momentarily forgetting that he had his phone in his hand. After a few seconds, he threw the phone toward his wife, but I'm pretty sure it was ruined by then.

Abby and Bosco, meanwhile, had decided that was enough excitement for one day. Plus, they were exhausted. Amazing Andy finally caught up to his chimpanzee and picked him up the way you pick up a newborn baby. "That's enough of that," he said to his baby chimpanzee. Then Andy glared in my direction. "I don't know who said you could bring that dog here. That was a big mistake."

Abby came over to me, panting hard. She looked up at me as if expecting a treat. And the sad thing is, part of me was so excited to see her acting so crazy. But that was a very small part of me, and it got even smaller when

Mrs. Lloyd walked over and said, "Obviously you and your dog need to leave. Please call your parents or your babysitter and have someone pick you up as soon as possible."

"Yes, ma'am," I said in a defeated whisper. I caught Daisy looking at me like, *What on earth were you thinking?*

I shrugged, picked up my dog's leash, and went inside the house to wait for Mrs. Cragg to pick me up.

I didn't even get so much as a single kernel of popcorn.

CHAPTER 18

THE CAR RIDE home was quiet.

I turned the radio on, but Mrs. Cragg said, "Now's not the time," and turned it right back off.

We rode in silence for a while, until finally I said, "I'm sorry."

She flashed the same look she gave me back when she was the meanest babysitter ever and made me eat kale and seaweed for lunch. "Sorry for what? Sorry for lying to me when you said Abby was invited to the party? Sorry for Abby scaring the daylights out of a poor defenseless little baby chimpanzee? Or sorry for ruining the birthday party?"

"The party isn't ruined," I mumbled. "It's going on right now. Without me."

My attempt at self-pity failed miserably. "Well, thank goodness for that," said Mrs. Cragg. "I hope they have a wonderful time."

"I'm sorry for lying," I said. "It was stupid. I just really wanted Abby to come with me because—well, because I just did."

Mrs. Cragg shook her head and clucked like a disapproving chicken. "Well, that's certainly a good reason."

"Did you tell my parents?" I asked. "Are they mad?"

"No, they're thrilled," Mrs. Cragg answered. "Who wouldn't want a son who doesn't tell the truth?"

I decided there wasn't anything good that could come out of saying anything else, so I shut my mouth. When we got home, Abby followed me quietly as I went inside the house—I think she thought she was in trouble too. I went into the kitchen and poured myself a bowl of cereal, then plopped down on the couch to watch some TV. I reached for the remote, but it wasn't there.

"Mrs. Cragg? Have you seen the clicker?"

"Yes."

I waited, until I realized that was her whole answer. "Can you tell me where it is?"

"No."

Oh, okay, I get it. So that's how it was going to be.

I went up to my room, Abby right behind me. I collapsed back on my bed and Abby climbed up onto my windowsill, which was her favorite spot. In the old days she used to jump out the open window when I went to bed and prowl through the night doing who-knows-what. But now she just liked to hang out there, watching the world go by.

"Well, Abby?" I said. "Everyone is mad at me—my friends, my parents, even my babysitter. And I can't watch TV. I'll probably be punished. But I got to see you run around this afternoon like the good old days, so you know what? It wasn't a total loss."

As I waited for Abby to answer, I decided to close my eyes for a second. It had been a long day. The next thing I knew, my cell phone was ringing. I groggily picked it up and looked at the time. 6:13! I'd been asleep for almost two hours! Then I looked to see who was calling.

DAISY F.

My heart did a tiny somersault as I answered. "Daisy?"

"No, it's me, Irwin!"

The somersault collapsed, and my heart went splat on the ground. "Irwin? What are you—why are you calling me from Daisy's phone?"

His voice sounded excited, almost out of breath. "Because we're all together at my house! Me, Daisy, and Baxter!" In the background I heard Daisy yell, "Hey, Jimmy!" and Baxter try to sound cool by saying, "Yo, what's up?"

"Oh," I said. "Well, how was the party?"

"That's why we're calling!" Irwin took a deep breath, like he was winding himself up. "We solved the case! We solved it!"

"What case?" I asked, pretending I had no idea what he was talking about. I started petting Abby, who was lying at the foot of my bed, and realized I was doing it to calm myself down, since I knew exactly what was coming.

"The Case of the Missing Presents!"

"Oh, really? I forgot all about that." *Yeah, right.* "Why, what happened?"

"Well, I was thinking after our meeting yesterday that if someone could come up with some sort of present that left a mark on the person when they picked it up, you could tell who the thief was," Irwin explained. "So I went down to the Magic Emporium and got this gag gift that when you open it up, you get sprayed with water, but then I went home and replaced the water with blue paint. And then I put a hole in the bottom of the box, so whoever picked it up would get drenched in blue paint."

I was confused—this time, for real. "Wait, I don't get it. What if there hadn't been a thief and Mara had opened it?"

"Yeah, I know," Irwin said. "That was a risk I had to take. Which is why I didn't say anything ahead of time. I figured you guys would've tried to talk me out of it."

Wait a second, I thought to myself. *I do something without telling the other guys and I'm a bad guy—but Irwin does it and he's a hero? How is that fair??*

"Well, I wish I'd been there," I said, which was pretty much the understatement of the year.

There was a shuffling on the other end of the line, and I could hear Daisy saying, "Let me tell him! Let me tell him!" Then another quick bit of shuffling, and Daisy's voice came on the line. "Jimmy, it was incredible! We were just sitting down to lunch before the show, and Irwin told Baxter and me about the exploding present. We all talked about it and decided that sometimes you have to be bold and take chances to solve cases, and the CrimeBiters are bold. We waited for you to come in because we wanted the vote to be unanimous, but after the whole Bosco-Abby thing we decided to go for it. So we were all watching Amazing Andy's show, and all of a sudden we heard this crazy scream, and everyone ran inside and there he was!"

"Who?" I yelled. "There who was?"

"Reptile Ron!" they all yelled at the same time.

"What?" I said. "Reptile Ron? You're kidding me!"

Daisy regained control of the phone. "I know, right?!?! He was standing there in shock. He was the only one in the house, because he knew that everyone would be out watching the show. He had a big garbage bag that was half full of presents, and he was covered from head to toe in blue paint! It was incredible!"

I was trying to process what I was hearing, but it wasn't easy. "I don't get it. You're telling me that Reptile Ron was the present thief?"

It was Baxter's turn to grab the phone. "Yup," he said, sounding much calmer than the other two. "It was pretty unbelievable. I guess when he says he's bringing animals back to their van, he's also sneaking inside and stealing presents. Someone asked him why, and he said he was tired of Amazing Andy getting all the glory and also he was a terrible boss. So Reptile Ron had this idea to ruin Andy's business by making it seem like presents were getting stolen at every party Andy was hired for. Then after Amazing Andy's business was ruined, Reptile Ron would take over."

"He was jealous!" Daisy yelled from the background. "And he couldn't take it anymore!"

Irwin yelled into the phone, which at this point was on speaker. "The whole thing is crazy, but the main thing is, we solved the case!"

"That's amazing," I said.

"Hey, what's the deal with you anyway?" asked Baxter. "Why would you bring Abby to the party?"

"Yeah, uh, good question," I said. "I—I guess I read the invitation wrong or something."

"What a bummer," Irwin said. "It would have been so awesome if you'd been there, but the main thing is that the CrimeBiters are back! Isn't that sick?"

"Totally," I said. "Hey, listen, I gotta go. I think I just heard my parents come in."

I hung up the phone and lay back down on the bed.

The CrimeBiters are back! Isn't that sick?

To be honest, I was feeling a little sick myself.

CHAPTER 19

SO YEAH, I was grounded. No big surprise there.

I believe my dad's exact words were "I wish we could go back in time before any of this happened, but I'm pretty sure that's not possible."

My mom's exact words were "Can I pretend we're not related?"

She was kidding. I think. But both my parents were pretty shocked—no, *really* shocked—at how boneheaded my idea was to bring Abby to Mara's birthday party, and they were also pretty disappointed—no, *really* disappointed—that I'd lied to Mrs. Cragg. So I wasn't just grounded. I also had to (1) write a letter of apology to Mara; (2) write a letter of apology to Mara's parents; (3) write a letter of apology to Mrs. Cragg; and (4) mow the lawn and rake the leaves twice a week and take out the garbage and empty the dishwasher every day and night for a month, which was probably the worst part of the punishment since it meant Misty didn't have to do any of those things.

The one thing they didn't do was tell me that I shouldn't do dumb things just to prove a point, because they knew they didn't have to. I was able to figure that one out all by myself.

So there I was a couple of nights later, emptying the dishwasher as usual, when I noticed a bunch of envelopes on top of the microwave.

"What's that stuff?" I asked my mom, who was standing next to me, trying to stop herself from helping me unload the dishes.

FACT: Even when moms punish you, they still want to help you. It's just in their nature.

"Oh, just the mail," my mom said. "I was about to go through it."

"Huh." I glanced at it casually for a split second, until something unusual caught my eye.

A bright-red envelope.

More like a *blood*-red envelope, actually. I picked it up and saw that it was addressed to Mr. James Bishop.

That's me.

My heart started to race as I flipped the envelope over, looking for the return address. There was none. But there was a cool sketched drawing of two black wings, and between the wings, where the body would be, were the letters *EE*, also in black, drawn in fancy script.

Elroy Evans.

"Holy smokes!" I hollered, so loud that my mom dropped the fork she was holding.

I ripped the letter open.

Dear Mr. Bishop:

I am in receipt of your recent letter.

First of all, I very much appreciate your kind comments. It is the goal of every author to create stories that move and excite people, and it is especially gratifying when children tell me that they have enjoyed reading my books, so thank you for that.

Second, you ask a very important question: How can you tell if someone is a vampire? That is an age-old mystery that I'm afraid may be impossible to answer. Part of our fascination with these extraordinary creatures is that we are never sure who they are among us, if they are in fact among us at all. It is possible that there are no vampires in this world at all, and it is possible that there is a vampire sitting at the very next table in a restaurant. This is the great unknown.

Third, believing in vampires most certainly does NOT make you childish. In fact, it makes you the opposite of childish. It makes you a dreamer. Someone who believes in possibility, and imagination, and the promise of something far beyond our natural beliefs and expectations.

And finally, Mr. Bishop, I would like to extend an invitation. As it happens, I will be in New York City in two weeks' time for an appearance and book signing at the annual COM-MIX convention. It is always a true delight for me to meet my youngest readers. As such, would you consider attending the convention, as my guest? And while you're at it, why not bring the creature whom you believe may be a vampire? This way, we can draw our conclusions together.

If this is something that interests you, please e-mail my assistant, Thora Saxby, at Thora@Evanstown.com.

I very much look forward to our meeting.

Most sincerely,
Elroy Evans

I sat down at the kitchen table, clutching the letter.

Holy cannoli.

I must have had some kind of crazy look in my eyes, because my mom came rushing over. "What is it? What happened? Is everything okay?"

I handed her the letter without a word. As she read it, it occurred to me that I'd never even told my parents that I'd written to Elroy in the first place. I hadn't told Mrs. Cragg either. The only person that knew was Misty, and she'd tortured me about it.

Boy, was it going to be *sweet* showing her this letter!

"Wow, this is amazing," my mom said, sitting down at the table next to me. "When did you write to him?"

"A few weeks ago, I guess. I didn't say anything because I figured nothing would ever happen."

"Well, something certainly did happen!" My mom got her cell phone out. "I'm going to call Dad. He'll love this! You're going to meet your favorite author!"

"What about being grounded?"

My mom waved me off. "This is a special occasion."

I was on a roll. "Can I invite my friends? Can Abby come?"

"We'll discuss all that tonight, but I don't see why not." My mom laughed. "Last I checked, there weren't any chimpanzees running around New York City."

I laughed too, probably a little too loudly. "Great! I'm going to go tell the gang!"

I couldn't believe my luck. The past few days had been kind of miserable—I was grounded, Abby was in the dog-house (not really, but you know what I mean), and the CrimeBiters hadn't even needed me to solve our biggest case in a long time. Now here I was about to tell them that they could join me in New York City to meet a famous author at the coolest convention in the world!

I went from feeling left out to feeling back in.

When I called the other CrimeBiters, they couldn't say yes fast enough. Baxter thanked me for helping him take his mind off worrying about his brother. Daisy said

"That is so awesome!" when I told her about the letter. Even Irwin sounded impressed, although of course he tried not to.

It occurred to me that I should have started writing letters to authors a long time ago.

CHAPTER 20

IRWIN WONK AND I have been best friends since as long as I can remember. He also happens to have the most awesome trampoline in all of Quietville.

The two things are still not related.

I still swear.

The day after I got my letter from Elroy Evans—my mom had already proudly taped it up on the refrigerator, which was the highest honor in the land—I was back at Irwin's, telling him all about the trip we had coming up to New York. As usual, I was the only one jumping.

"And after we meet Elroy, we can go out to eat at some fun place like an Applebee's or TGIF or something," I said.

Irwin rolled his eyes. "They have really delicious restaurants in New York," he said. "Like, from every country in the world. We could eat Tanzanian food, or Icelandic if we wanted."

"What kind of food is that?"

"I have no idea."

I kept jumping. "Maybe tomorrow after school we could all meet up and figure out what else we should do in New York. It's going to be the most fun day ever!"

"That would be awesome," Irwin said. "But, uh, I can't tomorrow. I'm busy."

"Doing what?"

"Just, you know, stuff."

"Oh, okay," I said.

I know what you're thinking—a normal person might have followed up with something like, *What kind of stuff?* But I wasn't a normal person right at that moment. I was a person who was way too busy thinking about how I was Elroy Evans's new best friend. I was kind of like a person planning his own birthday party. Nothing else mattered.

So you can imagine my surprise when I was leaving school the next day, heading toward the bus, and I saw a crowd of kids gathered over by the softball field. I craned my neck and was able to see some pom-poms flying around, so I knew it had to be cheerleading practice. But what could be so fascinating about cheerleading practice? I didn't need to see Daisy doing more flips and twirls, that's for sure. So I kept walking.

Then I heard a kid named Jack Winston yell, "No way! That is just so wrong!" which made everyone else laugh.

Okay, now I *was* curious.

I jogged over to the field. I could hear the cheer they were practicing:

"Put it in the basket. Put it in the hole. To shoot, to score, to win is our goal!"

I mean, it wasn't exactly genius poetry or anything, but there wasn't anything that sounded so wrong about that. And I didn't see anything else worth laughing about either, unless you counted the fact that Betsy Kincaid's glasses fell off every time she did a high kick.

Then I looked down the row of cheerleaders and saw something that made me rub my eyes.

I looked again.

Irwin.

As in, Irwin Wonk.

That's right, *my* Irwin. Neighbor, best friend, CrimeBiter.

And now . . . cheerleader.

Yup. There he was, right in the middle of the row, cheering his heart out. He was wearing an official cheer-leading sweater and a pair of shorts. He was holding pom-poms. And his glasses didn't fall off once.

He spotted me, and an embarrassed look quickly crossed his face, because he must have seen the shocked look on mine. He gave me a wave, then went back to work. Daisy spotted me too, and she grinned and yelled, "I know, right? Isn't it great?"

But before I had a chance to answer, Jack Winston hollered, "Yeah, it's great if you want to be a girl!" That inspired more laughter and a few other comments from the crowd:

"Hey, Irwin, where's your dress?"

"Can you do a split?"

"Who's the cute new cheerleader?"

I could feel my skin start to get hot as I watched Irwin try to ignore all the mean jokes. He just kept right on cheering. I knew I had to do something to defend my friend.

"Hey, everyone? Do me a favor and shut your mouths."

I wish it had been me who said it, but it wasn't. I wasn't quite fast enough, I guess. Or brave enough.

But Chad Knight was.

Chad stared at the crowd until everyone was quiet. Then he said, "I remember people made fun of me when I quit lacrosse to take up ballroom dancing. They didn't realize how hard it was, and how athletic. I bet it's the same with cheerleading." He gave Irwin a thumbs-up. "I think it's awesome that you joined the cheerleading squad. Keep up the good work. As for the rest of you," he said, looking around at the crowd, "grow up."

"I think it's great too!" I jumped in. "Way to go, Irwin!" But as we all know, nobody really pays attention to the guy who finishes—or speaks—second.

Chad came over and smacked me on the back, athlete to athlete. It kind of hurt, but I was going to keep that to myself.

"Very cool that Irwin is doing this cheerleading thing," Chad said. "When did he decide to join the squad?"

"A few days ago," I said. In other words, I lied. Irwin hadn't told me a thing, of course. And I knew it was probably because he thought I'd laugh at him, just like the other kids.

Since the fun was over, most kids started to drift away, but Chad and I stayed and watched for a few minutes, as the cheerleaders flipped and flew their way through a bunch of routines. It turned out Daisy *was* a really good athlete, and I was impressed watching her. Irwin, however, wasn't so great. But I could tell that he was having an absolute blast, and I'm pretty sure that's all that matters.

"You! You're the best! You! Can pass this test! You! You're the man! You! Can do it, yes, you can!"

The cheer ended, and Chad and I burst out in applause.

"Sweeeeet!" we hollered. "That was awesome!"

Daisy, Irwin, Mara, and the rest of the cheerleaders were grinning from ear to ear. Daisy might have taken an extra glance at Chad, but I didn't even care. They were my friends, they were having fun, Elroy Evans had invited me to be his guest in New York City, and everything seemed back on track at last.

Until the door of the school opened, and everything changed.

CHAPTER 21

THE FIRST THING I heard was a loud voice.

"NOOOOO!"

The cheerleaders stopped cheering, everyone stopped walking and talking, and we all turned to see Baxter, who had just come out of the school. Mr. Klondike, the vice-principal, was standing next to him with his hand on Baxter's shoulder.

Baxter was crying.

Irwin, Daisy, and I all sprinted over.

"Are you okay?"

"What's wrong?"

"Baxter, what is it?"

But he stared at the ground and wouldn't look up at us. Finally, after a few seconds, Mr. Klondike cleared his throat. "Can I tell them, young man?"

Baxter nodded.

"As I'm sure you know, Baxter has a brother, Bennett, who is heroically serving in our armed forces," said

Mr. Klondike. "This afternoon, Baxter's mother received word that Bennett was injured when the helicopter he was riding in had to make a crash landing."

A hard knot formed in my stomach, and tears sprang to my eyes. I looked at Irwin and Daisy, and I could tell they were feeling the exact same thing.

"Is he going to be okay?" I managed to ask.

Mr. Klondike glanced at Baxter, then back at us. "We certainly hope so. Bennett has been evacuated to a hospital where he will receive the very best care."

Baxter suddenly looked up. "My brother is the strongest person I know," he said, his voice sounding raspy. "He will be okay. I know he will be okay."

"We're here for you, Bax," Daisy said, and she wrapped him up in a big hug. Irwin and I stood there, trying to figure out what to do. Finally, desperate for something to say, I blurted out, "Do you still want to come to the COM-MIX convention with us? I really hope you do. But if you don't, we will definitely bring you back something awesome."

Daisy glared at me like I'd just asked Baxter if he wanted to see the inside of my eyelids, but Baxter nodded. "No, I still want to come. I have to ask my mom, but I think she'll say yes. It will be good to have a fun day in New York City."

I grinned. "Cool!" Then I looked at Daisy like, *See?*

Mr. Klondike pointed out toward the parking lot.

"Your mother is here, Baxter." Mrs. Bratford was getting out of her car and walking toward us, and Mrs. Cragg was with her. Mrs. Cragg was Baxter's dad's sister, which I sometimes forgot, since she'd become such an important part of our family too, as my after-school babysitter.

The two women reached Baxter, and it was clear they'd been crying too.

"We're all praying for your son, Mrs. Bratford," said Mr. Klondike. The rest of us nodded but didn't say anything. I quickly squeezed Mrs. Cragg's hand though. She squeezed mine back.

Mrs. Bratford tried to smile at us kids, then put her arm around her son's shoulder as they headed back to

their car. Mr. Klondike nodded at us before he went back inside.

That left Daisy, Irwin, and me all standing there. We looked at each other.

"I don't know about you," Daisy said to Irwin, "but I don't feel much like cheerleading right now."

"Me neither," Irwin said.

The three of us slowly walked home.

No one said a single word the whole way.

PART THREE

DROPPING THE BALL

CHAPTER 22

BAXTER ENDED UP being right—his mom did think it would be a good distraction for him to come to New York City with us and go to COM-MIX. So on the day of the convention, me, my dad, Baxter, Irwin, Daisy, and Abby all piled into the car and headed to New York. On the way there, we listened to an audiobook—*Fang Goodness*, of course, which was the first Jonah Forrester novel ever.

I could tell we were getting close to the convention center when I started seeing people wearing all sorts of costumes: everyone from Iron Man to Wonder Woman, Captain America to the Stay Puft Marshmallow Man from the original *Ghostbusters* movie—they were all there. We stared out the window of the car, suddenly feeling like weirdos because we were the only ones *not* dressed up.

We parked the car and walked a couple of blocks to

the convention center. I had Abby on a leash, and it was clear she was as fascinated by the costumes as we all were. There was a massive line to get in, but my dad pointed to a separate booth with a sign that said VIP/WILL CALL.

"You're a VIP, right?" he asked me. "Maybe we should go over there."

So we skipped the giant line and walked over to the booth, where two guards were keeping watch.

"Can I help you?" one of the guards said, in that way that meant *You people don't belong here.*

We stood there for a second, a little intimidated. "Uh, yes, please," my dad said finally. "We're here to see Elroy Evans."

"Elroy Evans?" the guard said. He and the other guard exchanged an amused glance. "I'm sorry, but you can't just walk in and ask to see the authors. And unfortunately, his signing is sold out. But you can still go over to the box office and buy day passes for forty-five dollars each."

"Is there a list or anything?" I asked the guard. "Like, for people who were invited?"

"Yes, we do have a VIP list."

I nodded. "I think I'm on that."

The guard raised his eyebrows but reached back to the table behind him and picked up a clipboard.

"Name?"

"Bishop. Jimmy Bishop."

He scanned down to the Bs, then stopped. He looked at me again, but this time there was a new expression on his face. I think it was respect. "Okay, here we are," he said. "Jimmy Bishop, plus guest." He glanced at our group. "Who's going to be your lucky plus one?" Then he looked down at Abby. "And no dogs, obviously."

Oh boy. I looked at Dad for help, but he looked back at me. "Your call, Jimmy." I didn't see how *this* could end well, but before I could say a word, Daisy and Irwin both said, "Take Baxter."

FACT: Sometimes best friends are true friends.

Baxter blinked. "Really, you guys?"

"Of course," said Daisy.

"We'll check out the other exhibits," my dad said. "Maybe we'll run into PancakeMan and get a picture with him."

"PancakeMan?" asked Baxter. "Is that a real superhero?"

My dad shook his head. "No, but he should be."

The guard gave me and Baxter two backstage passes that we had to put around our necks, then led us down the hall to a big room, where a crowd filled every inch of space. There was a blue curtain up front, and there—sitting right in front of the curtain—was Elroy Evans.

Elroy Evans!

A long line snaked its way around the room, leading up to his table, where he was signing books.

"Holy smokes," Baxter said. "Are all these people here to see Elroy Evans?"

"I think so," I said. A lot of people were dressed up like Jonah Forrester, who always wore a black suit, red shirt, and black tie. Some people were wearing fake fangs, of course. And a few even had the red leather gloves that Jonah wore in one book, *Fangs for the Memories*, when he had amnesia and forgot he was a good vampire and thought he was a criminal.

"Come with me, boys," said the guard who was walking us in, and we walked past all the people waiting and straight up to the front of the room, like we were copresidents of the United States or something.

"Holy smokes," Baxter said again.

When we reached the table, I noticed two other

people sitting next to Elroy. One of them I didn't recognize, but I knew right away that the other one was Nick Brindle, the actor who had played Jonah Forrester in the two movies they'd made so far.

"That's Nick Brindle," I whispered to Baxter, but he was too overwhelmed to hear me.

Elroy finished signing somebody's book and looked up. "Can I help you boys?"

The guard looked down at his sheet. "This is, uh, Jimmy Bishop, Mr. Evans. And his friend . . ."

PROFILE

Name: Elroy Evans

Age: Older than he looks in the picture on his books, that's for sure

Occupation: The greatest writer in the world

Interests: If I had to take a wild guess, I'd say vampires

"Baxter Bratford, sir," said Baxter.

Elroy twirled his pen in his hand and nodded, but he didn't smile. "Ah, yes," he said. "The boy who wanted to know how one could tell if someone was a vampire. That was your question, Mr. Bishop, was it not?"

"Yes, sir," I said nervously, as Baxter gave me a confused glance. Everyone on line started twitching impatiently, wondering who this annoying kid was that was slowing things down.

Elroy frowned. "Did you two travel all this way by yourselves? Where are your parents?"

"Well, my father is here, but he's waiting outside with my other friends and my dog, Abby. They said I could only bring one guest in with me."

"Well, that doesn't seem fair now, does it?" He gestured to the guard. "Lou, would you kindly find the rest of Jimmy's party and bring them in?"

"Absolutely, Mr. Evans," said Lou the guard. As he left, Elroy turned to the other people sitting at the table. "Jimmy and Baxter, allow me to introduce you to my partners in crime," he said. "This is Nick Brindle, who does me the honor of portraying Jonah Forrester on the big screen."

"We, uh, um, we know who he is," I stammered. "Nice to meet you, sir."

Nick chuckled and flashed a movie-star smile, which involved dimples and crinkly eyes and teeth whiter than snow. "Hey, fellas, good to see you. Glad you're fans of Elroy. Same here."

"Hey, Elroy!" yelled someone from the line. "We paid good money for this. Are you going to sign our books or what?"

The other guy at Elroy's table suddenly stood up like a shot. "Hey! Whoever said that, give him a minute!" he hollered, pretty aggressively. "He's visiting with friends! Be patient!"

There was some grumbling from the line, but no one wanted to take on Elroy's slightly crazy defender. I figured he was maybe Elroy's personal security guard or something, until Elroy pointed at the guy, laughed, and said, "And this one, making a strong first impression as always, is my son, Edison."

"I didn't know you had a son," I said.

Edison stuck his hand out. "Hey," he said. Then he did the same thing to Baxter. "Hey." His eyes kept scanning the crowd, still trying to spot whoever yelled at his dad.

PROFILE

Name: Edison Evans

Age: If I had to guess, I would say between 25 and 50

Occupation: The greatest writer in the world's son

Interests: Yelling at people on behalf of his dad

Elroy went back to signing, but the line didn't seem to shrink at all. After a few minutes, Lou came back in with Irwin, Daisy, and my dad, who had Abby on the leash.

"Oh, my word, you weren't kidding," Elroy said, eyebrows up. "If I'm not mistaken, that's a dog."

I was desperate to blurt out the whole story to Elroy— how I thought Abby was a vampire, but now I wasn't sure, and that's why I wrote him in the first place—but instead I just said, "Yes, Mr. Evans, that's my dog, Abby. She's awesome."

"She certainly seems it."

"Also, this is my dad," I said. "And my friends Daisy and Irwin."

Daisy and Irwin stood there like they'd forgotten how to talk. Irwin stared at Nick Brindle like he was a mythical creature come to life, which he kind of was. As my dad and Elroy shook hands, Lou whispered something in Elroy's ear, and Elroy nodded.

"Listen, Jimmy," he said. "It's great to meet you and your dad and friends, and it's especially great to meet your dog, but I've got some fans here who have been waiting a while to get their books signed. So for now, Lou's going to take you back to the greenroom area to get something to eat and drink while I finish up. Shouldn't be more than twenty more minutes or so."

"Wow, you must sign your name fast, Mr. Evans," Daisy said, scanning the tons of people who were still standing there.

"Oh yes, young lady," Elroy said. "When you've been doing this as long as I have, you learn a trick or two."

And then he sat down and signed about ten books in ten seconds. But the people he signed for didn't seem to mind. They clutched their books like they'd just won the lottery. And if you ask me, they had.

FACT: Greenrooms aren't green.

SO IT TURNS out that a "greenroom" is like a backstage waiting area for famous people to hang out and relax in, before they go onstage at a talk show, or out to a table to sign books. This greenroom was actually blue, but it was filled with tons of candy, tons of cookies, and tons of soda, which were three of my favorite food groups. And there was no one in there except us to eat and drink it all.

"Wow," Baxter said. "This is the *life*."

I put a cup of water down for Abby, who gulped it happily.

"Careful she doesn't have an accident," Dad said, but I wasn't worried. Abby was like a camel—she could hold it for hours if she needed to. It was kind of amazing. I mean, I don't want to call it a *superpower* or anything . . . I learned my lesson there . . .

We chomped and chatted for about ten minutes, until a woman came in. She smiled at us and sat down in a corner, where she put on some headphones and started bopping her head to the music. She looked barely older than my sister, Misty, but there was something about her that made me think she was a big deal.

"Is that somebody famous?" Daisy whispered.

"I have no idea," I whispered back. "But there's only one way to find out."

Irwin whispered, "What are you doing?" as I walked over to the woman and smiled. She smiled back and took off her headphones. "Hey, little man, what's going on? Is that your dog?"

"Yup," I said. "Her name's Abby. And that's my dad and my friends." They were all being shy—even my dad—but they waved.

"Nice to meet all of you," said the woman.

I helped myself to a fistful of peanut M&M's. "Are you a famous author?"

The woman laughed. "Ha! Well, it depends on what you mean by famous. If, by famous, you mean everybody at my mom's yoga studio has heard of me, then absolutely, I'm very famous." She turned around and handed me a copy of her book. "It's called *One-Forty*, and it's a graphic novel about a guy who only talks in one hundred forty-character statements. It's a commentary about how social media is running this country and ruining this country at the same time. But hopefully people will think it's funny too."

No one knew what to say except my dad, who asked, "Is your book for sale here? It sounds interesting."

The woman beamed. "Nope, but I can give you one, and I'll sign it for you too." She stuck out her hand. "My name's Sharona. What's yours?"

"Richard," said my dad. "But you can make it out to my daughter, Misty, if you wouldn't mind. She's so obsessed with her phone that sometimes I think her head is going to just drop right off her neck."

I watched Sharona open the inside of the book and start writing—I still couldn't believe that was a thing. Imagine getting a book signed by the actual person who wrote it!

My dad looked at what she wrote and laughed. "Check this out, you guys," he said, holding it up:

To Misty

  Reading beats tweeting any day!

  (Except when you're tweeting about how much you liked this book.)

  Your pal,

  Sharona Wild

"Wow, she's so lucky," I muttered. "She's not even here and she gets a book."

As we were rereading the words Sharona wrote, the door opened and Elroy walked in, with his son, Edison, slightly behind him.

"Where's Nick Brindle?" Daisy whispered to me.

"Shhhh!" I said, even though I was thinking the same exact thing.

"Where's Nick Brindle?" Baxter asked Elroy, nice and loud.

I felt my face start to get hot, but Elroy just laughed. "Oh, he's long gone. As soon as the last book was signed and the last picture taken, he was on the next flight back to Hollywood."

I saw Baxter's and Daisy's faces fall, and I was determined not to show the same disappointment. Besides, I was here to see Elroy—Nick had just been a happy bonus.

"It was so incredibly nice of you to invite us here," I said. "You've been my favorite author since, like, forever."

Elroy helped himself to one of the itty-bitty sandwiches they had on a tray. "Well, I wouldn't get to be an author if it weren't for my loyal readers," he said. "That's why I come to events like this, even though I have a fear of crowds. And when it comes to my youngest readers, such as yourself, it's especially important, because you are the ones who will keep my books alive into the future." He snapped his hand toward his son. "Edison, grab my bag from behind the couch, if you would be so kind."

Edison nodded, almost the way a servant would to a master. Then he scampered over to the couch, reached back, and grabbed a small brown duffel bag.

"Ah, yes," Elroy said. "Here we are." He opened the bag and pulled out three copies of his latest book, *Fangtango*. It was so new I hadn't even read it yet, but I knew it was about Jonah Forrester going undercover to break up a crime ring that was using a dance studio to steal people's identities and raid their bank accounts.

Elroy handed the books to Irwin, Daisy, and Baxter. "These are for you, and I'd be happy to sign them for you, if you'd like."

The three of them all had a look in their eyes like, *Is this really happening right now?* He signed the books, and they thanked him over and over again, as my dad looked on, smiling. I tried to smile too, even though both of my legs were jiggling with anticipation.

Elroy glanced at me with a twinkle in his eye. "What's the matter—worried you're not going to get anything?"

"Of course not," I said. "And I don't want anything anyway. Just getting to meet you is fantastic enough for me."

"HA!" Elroy said, barking out a laugh. "I appreciate the lie for the spirit in which it was intended." While I was trying to figure out what that meant, Elroy glanced at Edison. "The Vault, please."

Edison's eyes went wide. "The Vault? Are you sure?"

"Yes," Elroy said. "Very."

Edison looked upset, but he walked backed over to the couch, reached underneath one of the seat cushions, and pulled out a golden briefcase with the wings design and the letters *EE* stamped in big black letters, just like the envelope Elroy had mailed me. Edison looked at it, shook his head, and brought it over to his father. Elroy held it as carefully as you would hold a newborn baby.

"I call this briefcase 'The Vault,'" Elroy said quietly. "When I travel, I keep my most valuable possessions inside." He punched in a bunch of numbers on the lock, and the case clicked open. He kept it pointed away from Edison so he couldn't see what was inside. We all leaned in with anticipation, and Abby took advantage of the situation to stretch up onto the table and grab a hunk of cheese.

"Bad girl," I told her, but I didn't take my eyes off the case.

Elroy looked directly at me. "Jimmy. I mentioned earlier that young readers like you are the future," he said. "And to show my appreciation for your loyalty and

custom, I would like to present you with this signed, first-edition copy of my favorite Jonah Forrester novel, *Fangs for Everything*." He pulled out a big red book with a special gold-embossed seal on it and flicked away a speck of dust that was apparently on the cover.

Edison looked shocked. "Wait, seriously?" he asked his father. "For real?"

"That's enough, Edison," Elroy said, using the same tone that I'd used when I told Abby she was a bad girl. Edison scowled and grabbed a handful of pretzels but didn't say anything else.

Elroy held the book out to me. I didn't move. "Take it; it's yours," he said. My hands were trembling slightly as I took it, opened to a random page, and read:

Jonah Forrester felt strange. More alive than ever and blessed with the strength of a thousand men. After a lifetime of loneliness, he was determined to take advantage of his gift. If he was going to live in this world forever, he was going to do everything he could to make it a better place.

From that moment on, Jonah lived by one thought and one thought alone:

A vampire's job is never done.

"Thank you," I managed to whisper.

"Jeepers," Irwin said, with more than a hint of jealousy in his voice.

Elroy smiled. "Would you like me to sign it?"

I nodded and handed it back to him. He took a red pen out of his briefcase.

> *To Jimmy*
>> *Never stop reading.*
>> *Never stop thinking.*
>> *Never stop dreaming.*
>> *Your friend,*
>> *Elroy Evans*

I stared down at the words, trying to absorb the amazing thing that was happening to me.

"You better not sell it on eBay," Edison said bitterly.

Elroy hushed his son with a glance, then turned to me. "In your letter, Jimmy, you asked me how to know if someone is a vampire. Do you remember?"

"Yes, Mr. Evans," I said. I glanced down at Abby, who was parked under the food table, hoping for another snack. "You said it was an age-old question that was impossible to answer."

"Indeed," Elroy said. "Vampires are beautiful, and fascinating, and dangerous, and eternal. But most of all, they're mysterious. Jonah Forrester has lived forever, and how many people know he's a vampire?"

I thought for a second. "One."

"That's correct. His assistant, Saxton. Other than that, he operates in the darkness. That's the only way he can be effective."

Elroy smiled, and there was a hint of sadness in his smile, as if he knew that what he was about to say would disappoint me. "So my best answer is: If you think someone is a vampire, chances are they're not. Because most vampires would never, ever let you suspect a thing."

I nodded, and a weird, peaceful feeling came over me, as if he was saying what I knew to be true in my heart all along.

Elroy looked at his watch. "Well, I must be off. More books to sign, more hands to shake, more Purell to use. I've so much enjoyed meeting all of you."

My dad shook his hand. "My son will never forget this day for the rest of his life. You've been so kind. Thank you."

"It was my distinct pleasure." Elroy glanced over at his son. "Come along, Edison, we mustn't be late."

Edison hustled over to the door and held it open for his dad, and I felt a little bad for Edison—it seemed like all he was there for was to do whatever his dad asked.

After Elroy left, I stood there for a minute, just staring down at my book.

"That is, like, the coolest thing ever," Sharona said, from the other couch. I'd forgotten she was even there, but she'd obviously been listening the whole time.

"I know," I said, trying to sound calm. "Thanks."

"You know an actual vampire?"

"I don't know." I sighed. "I guess not."

The other guys sat on the couch and thumbed through their own books. No one said anything to me, as if they knew that I needed a minute to figure out the gazillion confusing emotions I was feeling. On the day I met my hero and he told me to keep dreaming, I realized once and for all that the dream I'd had about Abby wasn't true.

My dad came over and put his hand around my shoulder. "Quite a day. Should we go get something to eat?"

"Yes, please!" said the rest of the guys.

I nodded and slowly got up. Abby, who'd been snoozing, stretched and looked up at me with nothing but love in her eyes.

So she wasn't a vampire. She was still a great dog, and she was mine. That was enough for me.

"Let's go, Ab," I said.

And we headed back out into the great big world.

CHAPTER 24

I DOUBT THERE'S any place in the world that has more hot dogs than New York City.

That's because at every corner of every street, there's a man—well, not always a man, but almost always a man—standing at a little cart, selling them for two dollars a dog (which is a lot!). When we walked to the convention center, we must have passed at least twenty carts. And every time we did, the same thing happened.

"Dad, can we get hot dogs?" I'd ask.

"Not unless you want to die of food poisoning," he'd answer.

So, no hot dogs on the way to meet Elroy Evans. But when we left, the strangest thing happened.

We passed a hot dog cart.

"Mr. Bishop, can we get hot dogs?" Baxter asked.

"I don't see why not," my dad answered.

FACT: Parents might say no to you, but they'll probably say yes to your friends.

And just like that, there we were, eating New York City hot dogs. Can you get food poisoning from too much yumminess? Because those babies were *delicious*.

"Just be careful you don't spill any ketchup on your invaluable new possessions," my dad said. He meant our books, of course. But there was little chance that was going to happen, since I had my book wrapped in plastic, which was wrapped in Bubble Wrap, which was wrapped in paper, which was inside a shopping bag, which was tied and stapled at the top.

Abby stared up at us, searching in vain for scraps that didn't fall. I scratched her ear, but she didn't take her eyes off my meal. Dogs can have great powers of concentration when they want to.

My dad, who was the only one not eating a hot dog, pointed off in the distance. "See over there, you guys? About three blocks that way? That's Times Square. And the top of that building is where the ball drops on New Year's Eve. If you look, you can see the ball now, because it's there all year round. It used to be shaped like an apple, in honor of the Big Apple, which is New York City's nickname, but now it's just a big colorful ball."

We all squinted, especially Irwin, even though he was the one with glasses. "My parents let me stay up last year," he bragged. "I saw the ball drop; it was so cool!"

I tried to see what my dad was talking about. There were a bunch of giant buildings that looked like they went straight up through the clouds, and there were billboards and huge TV screens and more color and motion and activity than I'd ever seen in my life, but I couldn't find any building with a ball on top of it.

"I don't see anything," I told my dad.

"Well, maybe that's because of all the buildings in the way. Here, hop up on my shoulders for a sec."

"Okay." I put down my shopping bag, handed Abby's leash to Daisy, and climbed up on my dad's shoulders. He pointed again. "See it?" I wasn't sure I did, but I didn't want to be the only one missing this cool thing, so I said, "Oh yeah! There it is!"

"I've been coming to this city for about thirty years," my dad said. "And it never ceases to amaze me how gigantic and incredible it is."

"My mom always says New York City gets a bad rap," Daisy said. "She says that people think everyone here is mean and rude, and there's a lot of crime and stuff, but it's actually one of the safest cities in the world, and the people are really nice."

My dad nodded his head, which made me bobble on his shoulders a little. "That's absolutely true," he said. "The people here are the best."

It was between the words *the* and *best* when someone in a Jonah Forrester cape and mask came out of nowhere, darted up to us, grabbed my shopping bag off the ground, and took off—all in about three seconds.

Here's the crazy thing: we all watched the whole thing happen, but none of us moved. It was almost like we were watching a movie. There was no way someone just stole the most important thing anyone had ever given me! That couldn't really happen, right?

Except it *did* happen.

Finally, after a few seconds, my dad yelled, "Hey! Stop that person! They just stole my son's book!"

And just like that, somebody sprang into action.

Abby.

She took one look up at me, still on my dad's shoulders, and then took off after the thief. Of course, that meant that Daisy also took off, because she was holding Abby's leash.

"AAHHHHHHHHH!" said Daisy, in the split second before she and Abby disappeared around a corner.

Well, that was all the rest of us had to hear. I scrambled down from my dad's shoulders, and then we all sprinted around the corner too. The thief in the Jonah Forrester costume was still about a block ahead of Daisy and Abby, and they were all heading straight for the spot in Times Square where the New Year's Eve ball dropped. I hated that ball right then. If it didn't exist, none of this would have happened.

"Daisy, stop!" yelled my dad. "There are too many cars! It's dangerous!"

"I'm trying to stop!" she said. "But Abby won't let me!"

"Then drop the leash if you have to!" I yelled.

Daisy shook her head as she kept lurching ahead. "I can't let Abby run out into the street!"

This was it—the moment of truth. Did I believe in Abby? Did she have the ability to dodge traffic in the middle of New York City? *Was she a superhero crime-fighting vampire dog??*

I did. She did. And she was.

"She'll be okay!" I yelled. "Let her go!"

And so, at the corner of Forty-Second Street and Broadway—which my dad later told us was one of the busiest intersections in *the entire world*—Daisy dropped Abby's leash. Luckily, a policewoman on a horse spotted Abby running at full speed across the street, and she

managed to stop traffic. We ran across the street too, and suddenly we were in a part of Times Square where there were no cars. It was like a big outdoor mall, with people everywhere and tons of tourists taking selfies. And just like COM-MIX, there were tons of people in costumes: there was Elmo, Cookie Monster, Buzz Lightyear, Superman, Spider-Man, Batman, and, believe it or not, a man wearing nothing but underwear and a cowboy hat playing the guitar!

It occurred to me right then and there that New York was a pretty strange place.

My dad ran up to the policewoman on the horse, trying to get her to chase after Abby and the thief, who were still way up ahead. I wasn't sure the horse could get through the crowds to catch either one of them. But I wasn't worried, because I also knew how this would end.

I'd seen it all before.

In my dream.

"Come on, Jimmy, you have to do something!" pleaded Irwin, right on cue.

"We're all counting on you!" added Baxter.

I knew what I was going to say way before I said it. "It's all up to Abby now."

The bad guy still had my bag in his hand, and I wondered why someone would want a random shopping bag so badly that he would risk getting run over by cars and caught by a very angry dog with big fangs. But before I had time to think any more about that, I saw the thief weave around a family eating giant pretzels, hop over a little girl posing for a drawing, and run smack into the Statue of Liberty.

Or to be exact, a person *dressed* as the Statue of Liberty.

After being bowled over, the Statue dropped her (or his) torch, and it fell right on the thief's head, knocking him to the ground. Abby, meanwhile, jumped over a Bert, sprinted around an Ernie, scooted between a Mickey Mouse's legs, and pounced right on top of fake Jonah Forrester.

"Are you kidding me?" fake Jonah yelled. "What is she, some kind of magic freak dog?"

(Well, to be honest, I'm not sure those were his exact words, but since they were the words of the evildoer in my dream, that's what I'm going with.)

My dad, Irwin, Baxter, Daisy, the policewoman on the horse, and I all ran up to them. "You did it!" I said to Abby, giving her a big hug. "I knew it! I knew you could do it!"

She looked up at me, and I could swear there was a yellow glint in her eyes.

Hey, wait a second, I thought to myself. *Vampires have yellow eyes!*

"Look, you guys!" I said, pointing at Abby. "Look at her eyes! They're yellow!"

Irwin, who loved bursting my bubble any chance he got, pointed up at a giant screen towering over us, which was showing some weird random video of five bananas dancing. "It's just a reflection, Jimmy. Sorry."

But I didn't care. Abby was a hero, and now the whole city of New York knew it.

The policewoman walked over and jumped off her horse. "So this is the guy who stole your bag?"

"That's him," said my dad. "And that's the bag right there."

The policewoman took the bag and gave it to my dad, who handed it straight to me. I vowed silently that I would never let go of it again.

"Well, let's take a peek under the hood, shall we?" said the policewoman. She reached down to the perpetrator's face and flipped up the Jonah Forrester mask. We all gasped.

In a day full of twists and turns, this might have been the craziest surprise of all.

It was Edison Evans.

CHAPTER 25

"HEY, GUYS," EDISON said, from his position sprawled on the ground, with Abby still on top of him. "I bet you're wondering what I'm doing in this Jonah Forrester costume, stealing your bag."

Daisy was the first of us able to speak. "You could say that again, Edison," she said. "You ought to be ashamed of yourself."

The cop scratched her head. "Wait a second—you know this guy?"

"Yes, we do," my dad said, nodding. "He's a family friend. I'm afraid this is all a big misunderstanding."

I looked up at my dad. "He is? And it is?"

"Of course." My dad turned to the policewoman. "We're very sorry to have bothered you with this—I was just concerned for the safety of the children and our dog. Thank you so much for your time."

"Your horse is beautiful," Baxter chimed in. "It must be awesome getting to ride him all day."

"It is," said the policewoman. "But it's even better when people and animals don't go running through traffic because of a misunderstanding." She tipped her cap. "You folks have a good day now." She hopped back up on her horse, and they trotted away.

"New York's Finest," said my dad, nodding his head in appreciation.

I reached down and grabbed Abby, which allowed Edison to finally get up. "Thank you for not turning me in, Mr. Bishop," he said, wiping the city grime off his black Jonah Forrester cape. "That was very kind of you."

"I don't need your thanks," said my dad. "I need an explanation. You risked our safety with this little stunt of yours. What the heck was that all about?"

"Yeah, why did you steal my best friend's book?" Irwin added. "That was a terrible thing to do."

Baxter and Daisy nodded, and Edison looked like he wanted to crawl into a hole, which I would have happily dug for him. I was still so mad! But his face looked really sad, and really guilty, and I started to get a little less mad just looking at him.

"I'm very, very sorry. I don't know what came over me," Edison said. He was talking slowly, like he were trying to pull the words out of himself, as he sat down on a curb and stared up at the giant buildings all around us. "Did you know my dad based Jonah Forrester on me? It's true. I loved vampires as a kid, and so he started making up stories at bedtime about a vampire named Jonah, and I asked him if the vampire lived in the forest, and he said no, but his last name was Forrester. And the whole series came out of that. But I never got any credit, or money, or anything. And to this day my dad thinks of me more like an assistant than a son."

I thought about how Elroy talked to his son in the greenroom. It made sense.

"I guess I really grew to resent it over the years," Edison continued. "And then today, when I saw him give you that book, I guess I lost it." He looked at me. "Do you know he's never given me a first edition of any of his books? Not once. Elroy Evans is a hero to kids like you, and he's this amazing writer and everything, but you know something? He's not the greatest dad in the world."

Edison took a deep breath, as if he was exhausted. I sat down on the curb next to him. Neither one of us said anything. Abby came over and leaned her head on my lap, and Edison scratched the top of her head, which made Abby purr. It was hard to believe they'd been arch-enemies five minutes earlier.

"By the way," Edison said, "that's a pretty incredible dog you got there."

I smiled.

"I know."

CHAPTER 26

AFTER A FEW more minutes of Edison apologizing and us deciding to forgive him, he told us that he and his father were staying only three blocks away.

"It's the fanciest hotel in the city," he said. "Do you guys want to see it?"

"Sure!" we all said, before my dad could say no.

FACT: Some hotel lobbies are bigger than some small countries.

"Holy cannoli," I said—even though I still had no idea what that meant—as we walked into the lobby of the Hotel Magnifique. It looked like everything was covered in gold, including the grand piano that stood right in the middle of the marble floor. There were a lot of people walking around, but I can promise you that none of them were dressed like Elmo or Spider-Man.

"Come on up to the suite," Edison said. "You can see what six *New York Times* number one bestsellers can buy you."

"Can we, Dad?" I asked.

He sighed. "If I say no, will you listen to me?"

We got in an elevator—which was bigger than my bedroom at home, by the way—and headed up to the penthouse suite. The elevator doors didn't open onto a hallway with rooms, like a typical hotel— they opened right into the suite, which was *the whole floor.*

"Hello?" a voice called from a long distance away.

"Oh, wow," said Edison. He suddenly looked worried. "Dad's here."

Elroy Evans emerged from a room way down the hall. He had the same dismissive look in his eyes that he did earlier, in the greenroom, when he was ordering his son around. "Edison! I wondered what had happened to you. You shouldn't just leave like that. After the signing I came back here, thinking maybe you weren't feeling well." It seemed at first like he hadn't even registered there were other people with his son, but then he saw me. "My good-ness. Jimmy? Were you all together? What on earth is happening here?"

"Dad, I—" Edison began, but I interrupted him.

"We ran into Edison on the street. It was so funny! He told us he was staying in the nicest hotel in the city, and we begged him to show it to us. We're really sorry, Mr. Evans; we didn't mean to disturb you."

Elroy looked confused. "Please, call me Elroy. And you're not disturbing me, although, Edison, I do wish you'd checked with me first."

"No, Dad, that's not what happened," Edison said. "Jimmy here is just being nice."

I exchanged a glance with Irwin, and I think Daisy and Baxter exchanged one too. My dad shifted his feet uncomfortably.

Edison cleared his throat. "What actually happened is that I was upset that you gave Jimmy the first-edition book. So I followed them out of the convention center, to a hot dog stand where they were eating hot dogs, and then when they weren't looking, I took the book. I took it, and then I ran away. And Abby, this little dog, chased me all the way to Times Square and caught me." He let out a big sigh. "And that's what happened."

Elroy sat down slowly on a couch, as if he were about to lose his balance. "I—I'm speechless. You mean to say you stole the first-edition book? But why?"

"I guess because you've never given me one," Edison said in a clear voice.

Elroy's face went from angry to disappointed to sad, all in about three seconds. "I haven't?" he asked, mostly to himself. "Oh dear. I suppose I haven't." He looked his son in the eye. "I guess we have a lot to discuss."

"I guess we do," Edison agreed. Then Elroy put his hand on his son's shoulder, and no one said anything. I don't think anyone even moved, for like half a minute.

Finally I held out the book. "I would like Edison to have this," I said.

My dad smiled in a *That's my boy!* kind of way.

Edison smiled sadly. "I can't take it, but thank you."

Elroy didn't smile, but his eyes went from hurt to hope. "That is so kind of you, Jimmy," he said. "However, it is not your responsibility to help me and my son. It is up to him and me to understand what has gone wrong, and to fix it. And I make you this promise: we will."

Edison nodded slightly, then took a deep breath. "Nothing justifies what I did," he said. "I put everyone at risk, running through the streets of New York. I could have been arrested, but these nice people convinced the policewoman that it was all a misunderstanding." He looked at his father. "The least we can do is justify their faith in us by figuring out how to be more of a family."

"I couldn't agree more," Elroy said, and he hugged his son.

The rest of us all looked at one another, then at Abby, who was stretched out on one of the five Persian rugs on the floor, looking a lot like the queen she was. Then she got up and started sniffing around, like she wanted to make one of those rugs her own, if you know what I mean.

My dad and I looked at each other.

"We should probably go," he said.

CHAPTER 27

AFTER SAYING OUR good-byes to Elroy and Edison, Baxter pointed out one very important fact.

"We never even got to finish our hot dogs," he said. "I'm starving."

The rest of us looked up at my dad. He nodded. "I'm starving too," he said. "But this time, no lousy hot dog from a cart. This time, a proper meal."

So we headed to an outdoor café, where we tied Abby's leash to a table leg so she could watch all the people go by, which seemed like one of the main things to do in New York.

While we waited for the food, Baxter, Daisy, and Irwin talked excitedly about the events of the last hour, but I was thinking about something else. I was thinking about the last couple of weeks and how everything seemed connected.

"You know something?" I said. "A lot of bad things

happen when people feel jealous, or left out, or not appreciated."

All heads turned in my direction.

"Look at you, getting all deep," Irwin said.

"Yeah," Daisy said. "Where did that come from?"

"It's true." I took a bite of a nice hot buttery roll. "Think about everything that's happened lately. Reptile Ron was jealous of Amazing Andy, and he felt like Andy got all the glory, so he tried to ruin his business by stealing the presents. Edison was jealous of his dad's success and mad because his dad took him for granted and didn't appreciate him."

Daisy cleared her throat. "And when you helped make me president of the CrimeBiters, and I proposed having the meetings at my house, I think maybe you felt left out of that decision, and so maybe that's why you took Abby to Mara's party and tried to solve the crime all by yourself."

"Hey, yeah," Irwin said unhelpfully.

I thought for a second. Of course my natural reaction was to tell Daisy she was crazy, but somehow I stopped myself. Probably because I knew she wasn't crazy at all. She was exactly right.

"Maybe," I said, which was as far as I was willing to go—out loud anyway.

"It's not good to be jealous," Baxter said. "It's stupid and wrong." Say what you will about Baxter, but he definitely has a knack for getting to the heart of the matter.

The waiter came over with a tray full of food. "Here we are!" he said, placing my delicious fried chicken with macaroni and cheese in front of me. I couldn't wait to dig in, but as I was picking up my knife and fork, I noticed an extra dish on the waiter's tray. It was a giant steak, which I couldn't remember anyone ordering.

"What the heck?" I said. "Who's that for?"

The waiter put the steak in front of my dad, who quickly cut it up into small pieces. Then he bent down

and put the plate right in front of Abby. "A fair reward for a job well done," he said.

Abby stared at the steak for a second, like she couldn't believe her eyes.

My dad looked at me. I looked at Abby. "Okay, go!" I said.

She ate that steak in about four seconds.

I didn't say anything. I just gave my dad a hug.

"You'll notice I ordered it just the way she likes it," he said. "Extra bloody."

CHAPTER 28

MY DAD SAYS that Irwin, Daisy, Baxter, Abby, and I all slept the whole car ride home. I guess I believe him, because I don't remember a thing.

But I do remember driving up to Baxter's house.

And I remember pulling into his driveway and seeing about twenty cars.

And I remember Baxter saying, "What the heck is going on here?" as he got out of the car.

And I remember that even though it was late and everyone needed to get home, we all got out of the car too.

And I remember there was a big banner across their front steps that said WELCOME HOME.

And I remember thinking for a second, *Why would they make a big sign to welcome Baxter home from a day in New York City?*

But mostly what I remember is Baxter seeing the sign too, and starting to walk faster, and then jog, and then sprint up the walkway, and then throwing open the front

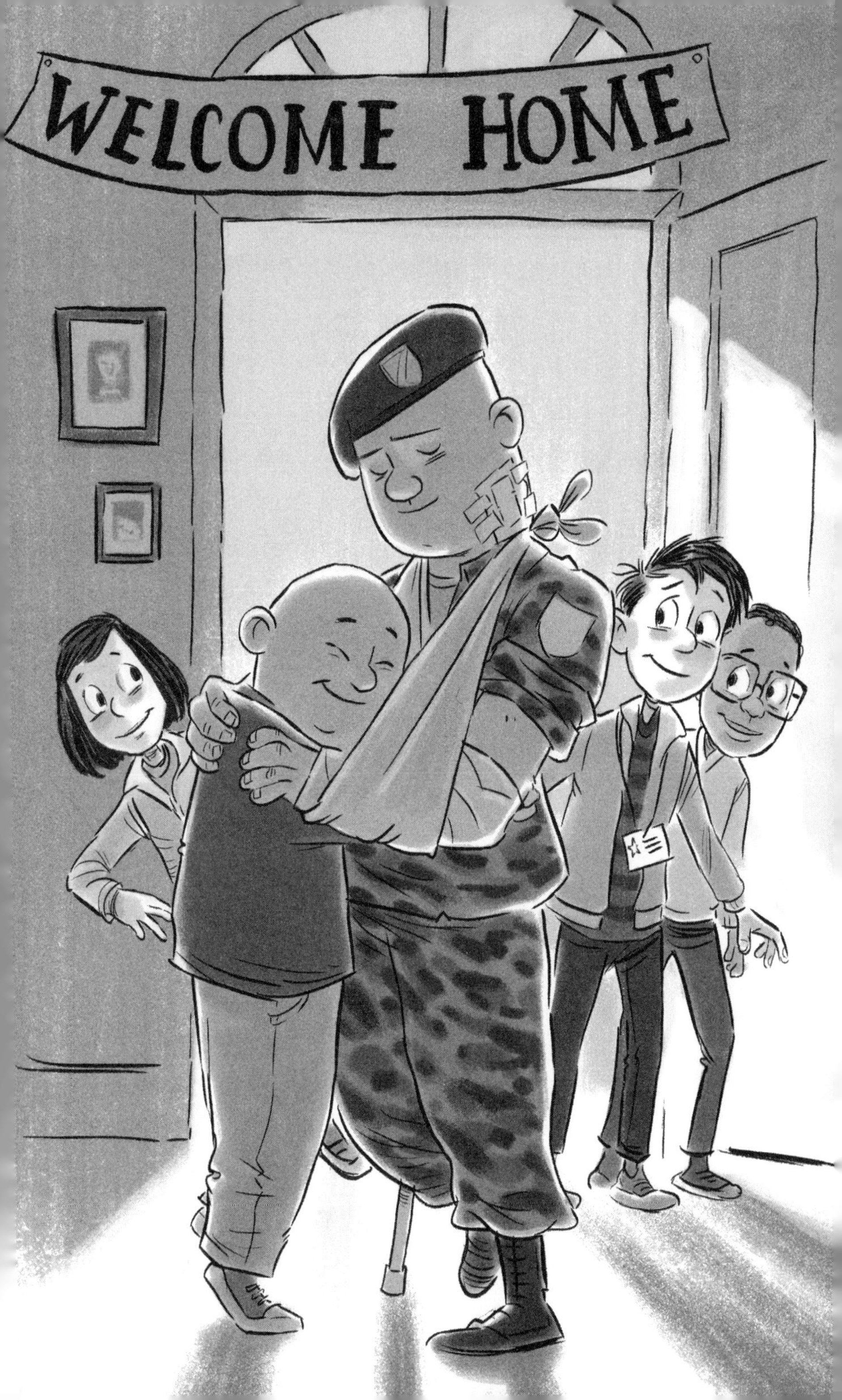
WELCOME HOME

door, and seeing his big brother, Bennett, standing there, with crutches, one arm in a cast, and a bandage on the left side of his neck.

And as the rest of us stood there and watched Baxter jump into his brother's arms, I realized that heroes come in all shapes and sizes, and some heroes are more super than others. You could be a vampire in a book. Or a boy who joins the cheerleading team. Or a Spider-Man walking around Times Square taking pictures with tourists. Or a dog who risks everything to protect his family.

Or, you could be the greatest kind of hero, the kind who has no superpowers at all—unless you count heart, loyalty, and courage.

EPILOGUE

FACT: Daisy's mom makes the best lemonade in the United States.

ANOTHER FACT: She also makes homemade ice-cream sandwiches. I didn't even know that was a thing. Ah-maze-ing.

FINAL FACT: A TV room is no place for a club meeting—no matter how delicious the snacks.

Is it too early to run for president again?

ACKNOWLEDGMENTS

WRITING THE CRIMEBITERS series has been a true joy, and a team effort. Going back to the beginning . . . I want to thank my wife, Cathy, who agreed to adopt a sweet puppy named Abby off the Internet sight unseen and then put up with Abby's tendency to stay active until the wee hours—the very habit, of course, which sparked the idea of writing a series about a vampire dog. I also want to thank my wonderful friends at Scholastic and Scholastic Book Fairs, who have been so supportive and skillful in bringing this series to spectacular life and into the hands of readers everywhere. And finally, how can I not thank Abby herself, who finally—FINALLY—has started to sleep through the night.

ABOUT THE AUTHOR

TOMMY GREENWALD AND HIS DOG ABBY

TOMMY GREENWALD is the author of the Charlie Joe Jackson series about the most reluctant reader ever born. Tommy lives in Connecticut with his wife, Cathy; their kids, Charlie, Joe, and Jack; and their dogs, Coco and Abby. Abby is not necessarily a crime-fighting vampire dog—but she makes Tommy and his family very, very happy, which is definitely a kind of superpower when you think about it.